I0760615

ALSO BY BOB STEVENS

FICTION

Dark Tales of Elsewhere

Dark Tales of the Inland Seas Region

POETRY

Dark Poems of the Inland Seas Region

Dark Poems of Elsewhere

from THE BOTTOMS FAMILY

Devil in the Pines

THE LAST ISLAND ALMANAC

jrefund no. 6 (2024)

Cover image by Heather Lee Shaw

Published by Mission Point Press
2554 Chandler Rd.
Traverse City, MI 49696
(231) 421-9513
www.MissionPointPress.com

ISBN: 978-1-965278-29-1(hardcover)
ISBN: 978-1-965278-26-0 (softcover)
Library of Congress Control Number:

Printed in the United States of America

BOB STEVENS

THE LAST ISLAND ALMANAC

Mission Point Press

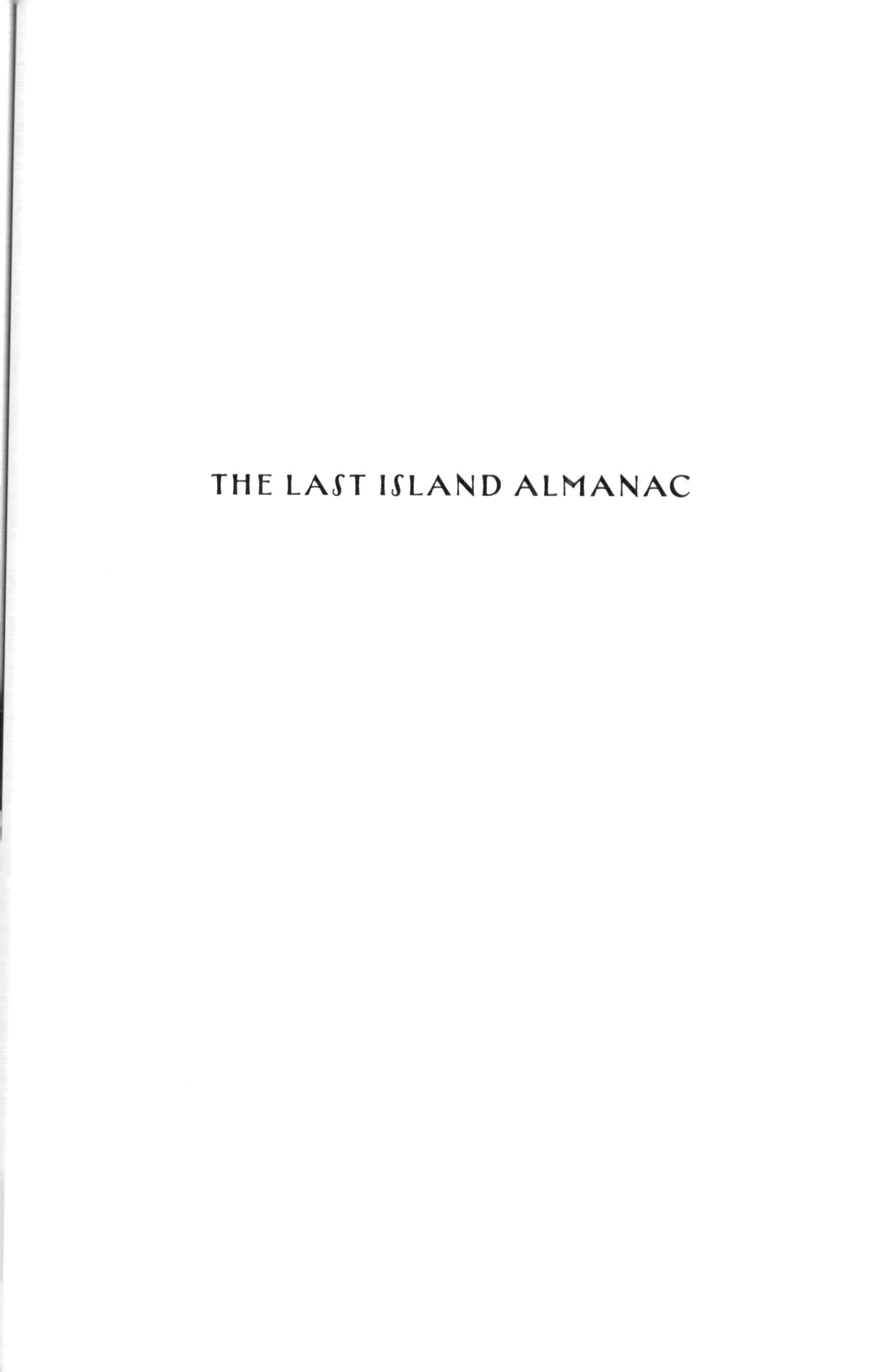

THE LAST ISLAND ALMANAC

DEATH ON THE RIVER OF DISCARDS

JANUARY 1

We are the only ones left, with twelve months to go if we make it that far. At least we get to die at home.

An older generation might remember the old slogan, "The River of Discards is my Home," on bumper stickers and T-shirts. I went through four of those. Sleeves rolled up and reeking of cigarette smoke. They somehow provided nourishment for a wounded pride. Truth is, past human contaminations aside, this is an area slowly returning to its natural condition—a scenic strait with strong currents, water with momentum and velocity actively being sucked down into the serene vista of Lake Bessie. She is the shallowest of the inland seas, and over a hundred lighthouses along her shores are testament to how tricky she can be to navigate. She also has sandy beaches and some notable port cities. Shipwrecks form reefs and rot in her bottom, and naval battles of cannon fire have been fought on her waves. The Island of Wendake, where we live—meaning my cat and I—lies at her northwestern edge.

Until recently, the River of Discards was a heavily navigated stretch. Long, slow-moving freighters with heavy loads of steel groaned in their passage. Sometimes you could hear the crew groaning, too—and sometimes, defiantly singing. Reliable assortments of smaller craft—from pleasure boats to rickety fishing contraptions with their sputtering outboard motors—always added to the water traffic. So did the border patrol and the coast guard. Not today. Today nearly all that water is locked in ice. It's been over two weeks since temperatures have been above freezing. Today the high was eleven.

But when the River of Discards does flow, it possesses a swirling energy hypnotic to watch. A litany of items floated down these straits over the years—damaged birchbark canoes, dangerously listing lumber barges, waterlogged corpses of those who leapt off expansion bridges, hula hoops and rifle stocks, photographs of children smeared beyond recognition, fur hats of drunken fur traders. A lot of these castoffs come from the historic City of Riverbend, just upstream. It is where water from the upper freshwater seas empties into the lower freshwater seas before eventually contributing to the ocean. Our narrow strait that flows westward for nine miles, then plunges south another twenty-four, was created by glacial retreat some fourteen thousand years ago. The contours of her path were forged by the scouring of ice sheets. The result of this scraping was not only a strait, but a sprawling assemblage of freshwater wetlands and marshes with over twenty islands along the way.

The Island of Wendake is the largest of these.

Facing my final year has got me thinking—should these

last days be spent moldering away? Shuffling through dusty rooms, carrying around empty picture frames? Stooped pathetic in my decrepitude, listening to forgotten songs on some outdated format? Coughing, wheezing, fading? Should my last breath be spent as a strange old man wallowing in memories in a strange old house where the icicle gutters hang crooked and the snow never gets shoveled anymore?

Doesn't sound very dignified to me.

Sounds goddamn terrible.

My goal is to keep things simple—keep writing every so often, but stay committed to living in the moment and only document events from the day just passed. I can no longer survive the presence of memories. They are too strong and I'm much too weak. So, nothing will be written about the past. No documents will be left behind. No photographs or journals. Nothing for the archives but this almanac.

This morning found me at the firepit in the cold darkness before sunrise, burning the things I kept the longest. It was horrible and draining and I'm all cried out. Those last things made an unruly fire. Not that anyone noticed. There honestly doesn't appear to be anyone around anymore. Sure didn't hear anyone out there today.

Everything was frozen and, besides the crackling of the fire, completely silent. Nothing but the occasional snap of ice resettling, a breeze off the river and through the trees, and the hiss of the flames vaporizing nearby snow as those final pages were fed into the heat—each flaring open in their death throes as if demanding to be read one last time. On a few instances I caught a name, sometimes more, before a devouring burn and a triumphant coughing of smoke sent them to oblivion. Sometimes a single scrap would lift defiantly on the scorching updraft as if propelled by some particularly compelling memory, but I was ready, poker in gloved hand, to pin those errant fuckers down.

Man-made fires have happened on the Island of Wendake for centuries, ever since various native tribes established seasonal encampments here. Birchbark canoes pulled ashore. Burning wood softly puffing smoke into starry evenings. The smell of cooked fish. The occasional cry of a hungry babe in search of a tit. And the husky tobacco laughter of clustered hunters with their lewd jokes.

There were elk and wolves on the mainland, harsh winters, and muddy springtimes. Mass migrations of waterfowl and overwhelming flocks of passenger pigeons. Then came paler faces with gunpowder, crosses, and the flapping dominion of flagpoles—first the French, then the British. Many-masted schooners dropped anchor. Again came the smell of cooked fish, and again the occasional cry of a hungry babe in search of a paler tit. But there were now homesteads in place of seasonal encampments, and farms and deeds and claims and paperwork. Much of the forest cut away to make room for one industry after another, from beaver pelts to shipbuilding, and later to iron and steel and chemicals. Through it all the Island of Wendake managed to retain a certain amount of dignity, but those various industries over the last two centuries precipitated a gradual darkening of the straits.

Things got ugly. The mainland was gashed with the stitching of railways and dominated by smokestacks and unending clatter. Shores were made of hard concrete and steel docks instead of marshes. With machinery clanking and smokestack clouds belching impurities, the River of Discards had turned sinister, and floating through on a hot summer night could feel like entering some watery hell-mouth with all the flames and combustion, red-reflected waters, clamor and racket. It was easy to imagine red-skinned demons, glowing like molten steel and dancing on those great piles of riverside coal, hiss-and-flare hooves scattering avalanches and throwing sparks into the polluted darkness. Things looked equally infernal when gazing down into the water. A blanching rot of fish with awful bulging eyes floated to the surface because toxic sludge was being fed into the strait through unchecked pipes. Fish also had to deal with the dredging construction of shipping channels on either side of my island—causing flow dynamics and morphology to be tragically altered, destroying breeding habitats. Thirsty animals wandered to the water's edge and gazed at the bubbling slop despairingly. Some of the thirstier and more foolish creatures took a sip and immediately hissed reddish steam, their tongues blistering, and keeled over. Death had unfortunately become the defining characteristic of the already grimly titled strait, and it was not the type of place most people wanted to visit. Vacations to the River of Discards became a punchline. Tasteless industrial waste postcards—skeletons waterskiing through sludge, deformed cartoon fish with too many eyes peeping through raw sewage, that sort of thing. And the people stuck living around here started getting sick from filthy jobs and defiled drinking water and the foul-smelling air.

"The River of Discards is my Home."

Thankfully things have improved. The straits now enjoy miles of restored habitat as the industrial corridor crumbles into rust-colored vapors and trees force themselves through graffiti rubble. Every now and then the ground shakes with bad memories or some buried pollution, but the landscape is overall much quieter. There are fewer smokestacks, fewer jokes. Over ninety species of birds. Sometimes things really do get better.

In addition to those birds, there are over a hundred species of fish slow swimming in the surrounding waters. Near the marshy shores you will find ambush predators like the muskie and the northern pike, smallmouth and largemouth bass, yellow perch, and bluegill. In the frigid depths tonight lurk fantastic and ancient lake sturgeon—primitive fish that have spawned here since the glaciers melted, leaving only for a handful of the most degraded years. The sturgeon have returned. Deep in the channel this evening, far under the ice, one just as old and heavy as me is hovering. Bony plates where other fish have scales, and cartilage where others have bones.

The Island of Wendake really isn't a bad place to die.

WINTER INTERLUDE

JANUARY 4

Heavy gales made the windows whistle and whine in the early morning darkness when my eyes opened, and for a moment, there was an illusion the entire house was creaking and swaying as if we had unmoored from the foundation and were getting tossed by the waves. My little house had been inexplicably swept off its slab and into the nearby straits, where it turned into a ship, and we tumbled along between big sheets of ice—dislodged in the thaw, marching off toward Lake Bessie. Me, the captain, with my lucky cat, the Lady Grimalkin, hanging on my shoulder—surrounded by the hungry sloshing of the water, just one big groaning creak and sucking whoosh away from going down forevermore.

Of course, we had not gone sliding away.

We were still on solid ground and my cat was resting peacefully in the turbaned pile of blankets at my side.

There was no rocking.

Nothing but the persistent wind and snow.

FIRESIDE ISLAND READING

JANUARY 21

With a knotty and unsteady hand, I reached out this morning and gave my lady a scratch. She stiffened, stretched, regarded me wearily. Then she wheezed and coughed, hopped off the bed, and wandered away. Having the Lady Grimalkin around is a consolation I probably don't deserve. Some days that cat is all that keeps me in the game. We've been through plenty. Ups and downs.

Besides my feline, the only other noteworthy companionship under this roof is books—thousands of books tucked onto shelves in every room. Some in better shape than others. Some hardbound and handsome. Some lurid and paperback. These pages are places I'm allowing myself to return to, and the books I'll be spending time with are old dog-eared favorites. Some haven't been off the shelves in decades, and of course, there is always the risk that one of them holds some forgotten ephemera tucked in the pages that will set off a torrent of debilitating memories. But I upend these at arm's length and give them a good shake before diving in—sometimes wincing, as if expecting spiders to drop out.

So far, so good.

The Lady Grimalkin enjoys days like this, days of reading. Whenever she senses me settling in with a book, my cat will position herself nearby to listen. She did so this morning. First on our reading list was a finger-stained and slightly water-damaged copy of *The Supernatural Guide to the Twenty-One Islands of the River of Discards*. It is a damn shame this precious volume, written by Rebecca Livingstone in 1964, has been out of print and unrecognized for so long. Damn shame she is now dead and our paths never crossed, especially considering we had several overlapping years living less than two miles apart. I know her house. It is on the still unpaved section of Hickory Drive, set back off the road and close to the canal. Candles lit the otherwise darkened windows at night when she was still alive, and smoke puffed from the chimney in all seasons. The old author was a notorious recluse, rarely seen outside. Eventually her curious behavior and interest in the supernatural secured her an unchallenged reputation as the island witch. Reactions to this fell neatly along the expected devotional divides. Rebecca Livingstone embraced it, routinely leaving broomsticks leaning on a porch where her various cats lounged and prowled. The picture on the dust jacket was taken when she was much younger. It captures her trademark disarming smirk, and her hair, the color of wet sand, looks windblown. This was someone comfortable in canoes. The brief dust-jacket biography claims she nurtured an elder's disdain for foolishness, loved casting bait for bass and walleye and, most of all, loved telling ghost stories. *The Supernatural Guide to the Twenty-One Islands of the River of Discards* contains twenty-one chapters, one for each of the islands.

The book begins with chapter one, "Drudge Island," a notorious industrial blemish she regards as the most preternaturally unstable of our islands and the one most darkly haunted. Unlike all the others, it is not a natural island. For the much longer part of its history, Drudge was nothing more than a marshy peninsula at the mouth of the Lower Osprey River—a haven for waterfowl and snakes and mosquitoes. Local tribes, for thousands of years, used these two hundred acres of marshland for special burials. Herons nested above the bones, a sulfur spring bubbled foul-smelling mineral water, waves lapped at the decomposing shore, and spirits occasionally wandered. Then the area was purchased by the wealthy Samuel Drudge in the latter half of the nineteenth century. Drudge was a political progressive and devout churchgoer who imagined a secluded estate in those marshes for himself and his wife—a place to test his rifles on ducks from his own rambling porch, to praise his creator for the bounty provided, to hail the sunrise over the water. But living on the peninsula soon proved intolerable. According to Rebecca, it was not only the smell of the sulfur and the insects, but the chattering disembodied voices and the shuddering hiss of ghostly arrows that kept him awake and uncomfortable. He was so angered by his failed riverside estate that he spitefully sold the property to be used as an industrial dumping ground, and when a shipping canal for countless tons of sludge was excavated, this devastated marsh officially changed status. Surrounded by dirty water on all sides, she had been carved into the most dismal island imaginable. Far from the idyllic resting place and wildlife sanctuary it used to be, rat-infested Drudge Island is further contaminated by the disrespected dead, and those living directly across the straits have complained that it often emits a preternatural humming sound.

After "Drudge Island," I skipped ahead to the fourth chapter and read the brief but lovely little ode to the always modest, and now completely submerged, Mamajuda Island. When above water, it was over twenty acres large and boasted a red lighthouse with a fixed light. Currents could, of course, prove dangerous, but the adventurous Rebecca Livingstone paddled there many times all by herself. It has always been a good place to catch bass, especially in the month of May when the white bass joins the dependable smallmouth and largemouth in an overlapping frenzy of mating and laying eggs. The white bass is the most gregarious of the three, often found schooling and feeding near the surface. These energetic beauties have the hunched appearance of an ashen salmon, lower jaws protruding beyond their snouts. More of a big-lake fish, they only come to the gravel shallows of Mamajuda when spawning, and that is where Rebecca Livingstone recalls catching them in great numbers. Little clusters of boats would build up on the water there every springtime, hauling in feisty beauties of eighteen inches and up to two pounds. She spends a full paragraph on her own fishing success in these waters, then transitions into the tale of a ghost maiden pulling translucent bass, one by one, from a placid unblemished surface in the moonlight. She relays the tale as a firsthand witness and assumes Mamajuda is the name of this radiant maiden, and this is *her* island. Rebecca claims the spirit beamed an overpowering benevolence, all hospitality and kindness. Hers was a smile that said this is a fine place for a woman to be alone and away from the bullshit world of men. It was a smile that said you have come home. The fishing here is good. Then, as Rebecca tells it, the lovely maiden blasted apart in an auburn light that spilled liquid into the waves and sent a legion of ghost fish, fins rippling in expanding concentric circles just below the surface, until they made it all the way to the small rowboat where the author was seated. They filled the planks beneath her with an unaccountable warmth, a familiar warmth that carried with it the aroma of a pregnant river after a strong rain. She nearly swooned and toppled into the water, but managed to keep upright and begin paddling. In the confusion of the moment, however, she had advanced aggressively in the wrong direction and found herself helplessly drifting too close to the rocks where she was forced to land and pull her canoe ashore. Fatigue overcame the author and she laid down to rest.

She claims to have been awoken with a shoulder shake by the lightkeeper's daughter, a girl around her age who henceforth became a lifelong friend. The girl and her family eventually had to leave. The thirty-four-foot-tall lighthouse, victim to the eroding wake of passing ships, washed away. The whole island disappeared, save for some scant water-lapped boulders, just ten years later. It is now nothing more than another submerged section of the much larger Mamajuda Island Shoal, resting about seven feet beneath the surface clear up to Bluestem Island. Presumably the maiden assumes an altogether more ghostly rime glimmer on deep chill evenings like tonight. If only I had the strength to walk up there to see for myself—but it is much more responsible to read safely by this fire, with this cat. Besides, it's snowing again, blowing into the window and gathering at the edges. Mamajuda Island is under ice and out of the question.

I then flipped to another account involving loss of consciousness—chapter nine, "Fawn Island." Here Rebecca drifts farther downstream to an uninhabited seven-acre refuge that rests quietly a thousand feet west of the southern tip of Wendake. The main attraction of this place is that no one lives there. No one has ever lived on Fawn Island. Just a lot of birds. If you prefer the company of snowy egrets and canvasbacks, and even the passing common merganser, then you may want to take a slow paddle around those hissing shoreline willows once it warms up. During migration months, the reward of a quiet approach is a chorus of resting songbirds in the hundreds. Fawn Island also enjoys her own distinct spirits. Rebecca, when she was a precocious fourteen-year-old tomboy, took the family boat out there one late June afternoon to prowl the shores with a fishing pole and a transistor radio—secretly disembarking from the family dock on the canal with her brother's tackle box. There were five hours left until sundown, usually more than enough time, but she would not make it home until well past dark. Rebecca claims the first indication of inexplicable forces was the sputtering of that radio. More than sputtering, it seemed to be trying to belch out syllables of meaning through the static. With a big shiver, she leaned over and turned it off.

Then the motor wouldn't start.

In eleven feet of water and drifting farther toward shore, the damn motor wouldn't start. The lapping waves mocked her. Something unusual was underway; something was about to happen. The tension increased as the water became shallower. A supernatural force was mustering itself with the setting sun and invisible hands gently tugged her boat to shore. She said it felt like the island was tucking her in. As the tip nudged into land she was overcome with drowsiness and had no choice but to make a comfortable spot and nap. She does not provide details of all the dreams she had, but says enough to suggest there is a spirit of romance that lingers in that wild place. She awoke hours later with a white streak in her hair and an aching in her privates.

The last chapter I was able to read today was number fourteen, "Little Wegobemish Island." It lies on the other side of the tip of Wendake from Fawn and, at thirty acres, is considerably larger. It also has a much different history. Unlike the isolated and mysterious Fawn, for over forty years Little Wegobemish Island trembled with human activity every summer, because up until 1936, this was the location of the Little Wegobemish Island Amusement Park. Forty years isn't a very long life for an amusement park, but apparently just long enough to spawn a haunting or two. Rebecca Livingstone had childhood memories of the place. She knew the height of spectral activity would fall in the warmest months because once, as was proudly scripted across their promotional posters, Little Wegobemish Island Amusement Park was "The Place Where Summertime Memories Are Made." Most of these memories were fine and romantic, but the little remote park also had her share of tragedy. With so many people passing through for so many hazy summertimes, a few random deaths by drowning and jealous lovers and roller coaster derailments were bound to happen. So many people, thousands passing through. Most were thrill seekers from the big city of Riverbend who were floated down the straits on a cheerfully puffing steamer trailing perfume and calliope music and tobacco smoke and laughter. For nearly all those years, the steamer in question was the *Ashen Belle.* Her passengers journeyed downriver to escape. They came by the boatload to fall in love and get drunk or get drunk and fall in love. You were treated to a live orchestra, playing in the middle of a hardwood pavilion dance floor lit by lanterns. Dancing was free. There were shaded picnic areas and a boat livery where city dwellers could, at moderate rates by the hour or day, rent a rowboat to slap paddles through the surrounding waters in search of fish and scenic beauty. Every summer for all those years, Little Wegobemish Island drew in thrill seekers and absorbed their spirit.

Then hard times hit and the place was abandoned to the slow demolition of nature. No one laid beach blankets on the sand anymore. The roller coaster tilted sideways under the weight of muscular vines and eventually toppled during a summer night of intense thunderstorms. When fall arrived and the sugar maples dropped their orange leaves across the damaged pavilion, you could sometimes see the twirling tops of coupled dancers—twirling and transforming to skeletons still twirling. The rusted wreckage of the roller coaster is getting buried in the snow tonight and the *Ashen Belle* is gliding along through the ice as if there were still waves to ride, smoke writhing from her twin stacks. She will wake no sleepers when she vanishes into the quiet shore of her long-ago destination.

My day of literature continued and stretched into the

evening. After lunch, the Lady Grimalkin followed me back to my reading chair, and, for both her enrichment and mine, I flipped through my copy of *Snowbound Along the Salteaux,* by Celia Vermette, and alternated between reading passages aloud and to myself, although, in her preternatural way, it seemed as though the expressionless Lady Grimalkin heard both just as well. I read descriptions of blizzards and cannibalism, and she curled up to fall asleep and dream of blood and snow. Then I put the Vermette back on the shelf and slid down the volume next to it—*The Bellsnickle and Other Legends of Lake Manitou,* by Anthony Selfridge. From these pages sprang tales of the bellsnickle—loathsome bogey of the yuletide, dragging his bulging sack of sorrows across the white landscape of the holiday season. Included in the first chapter were detailed and ludicrous methods to avoid his detection and disapproval. Selfridge also documented shipwrecks that were the result of witchcraft, and certain stretches of boreal forest where the fabric of things had the habit of falling away. The result, in his words, was a transfiguring glimpse into the infinite. The best chapter may be the one on Cauldron Lake.

The Lady Grimalkin yawned and rolled over.

She had heard all of this, way too many times before.

THE LADY GRIMALKIN

FEBRUARY 5

This morning she was sniffing my face, nervously testing me for signs of life.

When shallow wheezings were detected and my eyes opened, she slouched back with a visible unraveling of concern. I had apparently been holding my breath in my sleep because I came up gasping. The air felt heavy and muffled and cold.

The Lady Grimalkin meowed.

I sniffed and sat up.

"I'm still here," I told her. "One day it will be clear I'm giving up—I will probably tell you—but today I'm still here." She meowed again, this time louder, and, like most cats, she never makes such a racket when content. Different pitches, so I've learned over the years, signify different sources of displeasure. This morning the empress meowed in a very conversational variety of voices, indicating a litany of issues that needed immediate tending. I gave her a scratch on the top of the head which she haughtily withdrew from—serpentine tail flicking, creating cursive admonitions in the thin air.

She needed something.

She meowed even louder at my groaning struggle out of bed and sauntered off on her own sore bones, demanding I do the same. She had a legitimate set of grievances. In the kitchen I found both her water and food bowls empty, joined together by the shameful mockery of an undulating spiderweb. A glance at her litter box revealed a mess. I had an overwhelming sensation of somehow having been asleep for more than a day. The world outside the laundry-room window was covered in fresh white snow. I felt famished and ashamed.

"Poor Lady Grimalkin, poor sweet Grimalkin..."

I was saying this when I stood up to get her food off the shelf and nearly stepped on a dead white-footed mouse. Poor thing looked like many of the other mice left for me to discover over the years—deflated somehow, flattened by paws and exhaustion and blood loss, its tiny rodent mouth rigid and gaping. The tail on today's victim was missing, presumably devoured or batted away under something by playful paws. It had been bitten and scratched significantly before being put out of its misery, though.

Cats.

At least her hunting has been reduced in the more rigid scowl of her advanced years and it's increasingly rare for me to find dead things around the house. Poor kitty has a hard time catching anything at this point. The dead mouse lying at my feet must have already been in decline. I looked over at the Lady

Grimalkin and found her watching, a bemused smile curling her lips back to show off those canines, and then a wink. An undeniable flirty black-cat wink. Momentarily a smoking cigarette extended from her mouth on a long holder and she puffed in murderous satisfaction, as if to say, "I wouldn't have to do such things if you kept my food bowl full, sailor."

Then the vision dissipated and my companion was restored.

She continued watching me, viewing the inspection and removal of the dainty carcass with an aloof licking of her paws. Her breast heaved out. She straightened her back. She has always been a proud feline, and these types can be the most rewarding to share a house with. They provide you with daily examples of carriage and grace. They remind you how to relax. They make you feel privileged.

"What an extraordinary hunter you are."

She stopped her licking and looked up, curious. Then with a lowering of eyelids her mood darkened.

Cats have a haw, or third eyelid.

A lot of animals have them.

In some this haw is translucent, and in others, just transparent. Working like a windshield wiper, it can sweep across the eye, cleaning and lubricating. But for my cat, in her role as predator, this haw serves the additional purpose of protecting her vision when attacking.

"Such a ferocious predator, sweet sadistic Lady Grimalkin, bloodthirsty geriatric, benevolent queen, so sorry I fell asleep for so long."

She softened her stance. She likes hearing me talk in that particular tone, responding with approval to anything that comes out slowly, anything that comes out dripping in honey. For her it is an indication that she has secured my undivided attention. I leaned down and kept spooning out the sweetness until I heard purring. Cats begin purring as kittens and are typically loudest when milking. An entire litter latched on and humming in unison when the mother joins them is the loudest purring you will ever hear—the sound of impossible familial happiness.

Black cats, with their heavily superstitious branding, are my favorite. The ascending witch with feline familiar elegantly balanced on her broomstick. People shrinking back in terror as some gaunt midnight stray leaps unexpectedly out of an alleyway to cross their path. Ladies heading to church, crossing themselves at the sight of some pussycat all spread-eagled and licking her furry privates on the side of the road.

Black cats are the best. Most animal shelters have a few. They still get passed over by most folks. The Lady Grimalkin had been at the shelter for months before we came in and claimed her. Although it is worth mentioning that her previous owner must have been someone with diabolical tendencies because, while the Lady Grimalkin has never had any behavioral problems, she does have the fascinating habit of hissing whenever she sees a crucifix. There was only one left in the house when she arrived, anyway. It is now kept in the tool closet in case of vampires and only pulled out every so often to test her. She is never pleased. I get a hiss and an arching back every goddamn time. The sensitive beast is often in a foul mood for hours after such an affront and the only way to return to her favor is by handing over some treats and hauling out the compliments. I lean down to tell her she is an elegant transgressive; a gloriously unholy priestess that hisses, ears pressed; a furred emissary sent with whiskers twitching and trailing sulfur from the pit; a sweet blackened hell-spawn with faraway eyes, always on the verge of the lewd, always on the verge of the downright sinful. You are adored. Meow.

It is certainly true that black cats are forever associated with exceptionally *bad* luck, but there have been exceptions—the most notable being the beliefs held by sailors. For many who took to the sea, the presence of a happy cat on a ship was essential to good fortune. The initial purpose of bringing them along was to contain any rodent problem, but these nautical cats soon attained a more rarified stature and hunting skills alone cannot account for the lengths to which they were pampered and shielded from harm. Sailors were fearful that cats could control the weather—the happier the cat, the more pleasant the seas, is what many of them believed. Men whose faces bore the flecks and facial strain of long seasons spent leaning into waves and wind, hearty and stern men of premature wrinkles who were tough as nails, were not above tenderly filling a bowl with milk and providing well-placed scratches and gentle strokes. These sailors worshipped cats and to visit any bodily harm on them was a serious taboo. Following a perceived slight, the beast might grow inconsolably sullen and the weather would take a blustery turn for the worse—calamity gales and foamy crests, capsizing and casualties. Just for messing with the damn cat.

Other stories exist of an abused feline doing the opposite and charming the seas to lifeless tranquility without any wind or waves at all. Sails hanging limp for weeks and food rations diminishing. The becalming cat, perched on a pile of ropes, lethargically cleaning her paws.

EASTERN WHITE PINE BIRD-WATCHING

FEBRUARY 11

It snowed again last night. Nine inches total. Even the old truck would have been hard pressed to rumble over what is now a foot-high snowpack. Adding to the difficulty is the quality of the snow. This most recent round was different from the lake effect and clipper fluff we'd been getting the last week or so. It was not one of those light sparkle snows, but instead an onerous and damp accumulation, perfect for snowballs but hell to shovel. All last night and into the morning it tumbled down in curtains of slanted white, piling up for a good seven hours. A man my age can't be expected to remove that mess. So, there it all sits. Fuck it.

I keep hoping to hear the heroic roar of a snowplow, but damn if this place doesn't feel abandoned. Haven't even heard a single snowblower. No scraping of shovels. No belligerent salt-truck rumblings.

Doesn't seem to be anyone left to come to my rescue.

Consider the evenings.

Everything stays dark.

Only one house, in fact, seems to have any electricity at

all. Unfortunately, those lights are *always* on, like the inhabitants are all lifelessly slouched inside. Tonight, however, it emitted only the faintest glow. Maybe there is only one working lightbulb left in the place. Maybe all the other lightbulbs, recognizing the futility of their illumination, agreed to flicker out in unison. Except for this one. Snowfall only increases the desolation.

There was a little episode this morning—an odd popping in my chest, coming directly after the minor exertion of cleaning the shotgun. Should probably get that old revolver out of the safe and do the same. That's what I was thinking when I put the shotgun away and took a break in the bird-watching chair by the big picture window, geriatric blanket tossed like casket draping over my lap, sunken face as pale as the storm, blood pressure plummeting, perhaps. Guess I've been pushing myself too hard. It would be a big disappointment to die this early in the year. From now on, I'll stick to even easier things than shotgun cleaning, like bird-watching.

Three different feeders can be seen from the picture window—a hanging suet cage, a dangling cylinder with tiny brass perches filled with an assortment of seeds, and a platform feeder. They are all arranged beneath the most prominent feature of the backyard—a fifty-foot eastern white pine. My favorite tree. Great tree for a bird-watcher to have. It guarantees you nuthatches and chickadees, and then word gets around quick.

The pine sits on a small hump in the backyard, branchless for ten feet off the ground, and has perfect posture all the way up. She faces the buffeting winds of the straits like the mast of a ship and is already assuming her mature configuration of branches, top heavy and spreading outward. She could easily live another hundred years, probably more.

Winter is her best season.

Snowy landscapes suit her.

The feeders arranged at her base were my only destination today outside the house. I'm running out of seed, but had enough to fill all three. Birds always descend by the famished dozens after a big, heavy snowfall. Four black-capped chickadees arrived first, hopping with happy dinner-bell calls, letting everyone know. They were quickly joined by the tufted titmouse. Both are year-round residents. Sometimes they are the only two types of birds braving the enticement of my feeders in a full-blown winter storm, but if a third is to join their blizzard party, it will be the dark-eyed junco. Juncos are true deep-winter birds who only visit our island from November to March. Tough little balls of energy, they mingle in nicely with the chickadees and the titmice, preferring to feed on seeds fallen to the white below. All three species respectively peck together, weaving in and around with spastic decorum. The Lady Grimalkin used to lock the slits of her eyes on these creatures and squat herself into pouncing position but the years have muted her interest. The spirit of the huntress that once possessed her has faded, reducing her to the passive status of bird-watcher, like me. Every so often you might catch a flash of hunger in her predator eyes, but mostly she seems to have matured into a dumbstruck fascination with her former prey. At a certain age all you can do is sit back and watch, which is exactly what we both did today.

We most unexpectedly sighted a brown creeper. This unusual bird has the telltale habit of landing at the base of a tree, from where it will climb—up and up against gravity—in search of tiny invertebrates nestled under the bark. It was doing this on the trunk of the white pine. They prefer thick and sturdy old trees, especially in dampish woodlands near larger stretches of water. Makes sense they would be here. I wish I could tell you that this particular brown creeper stays with me all year round but she is only a winter visitor, maybe even from the shores of Lake Manitou. In summertime there is an entirely new population of creepers who come here to nest and breed. These breeding pairs, however, are even more mysterious and rarely seen—shielded by the lush shadows of a warmer season and busying themselves with the clandestine duties of tending to eggs and hatchlings. Their nest, constructed of woven spider silk and conifer needles behind the dislodged bark of dying trees, is notoriously difficult to find.

(4:45 p.m.) Not long after the brown creeper flew off, all the

other birds scattered, too, and a hawk appeared—perched impressively on the telephone pole in the back corner of the yard. It was a female northern harrier, full grown and nearly two feet high. She surveyed the silence, then flapped down to the surface of the snow to preen and rest awhile. The Lady Grimalkin and I both arched our backs in interest. Such prolonged viewing of a marsh hawk like this is a rare privilege. Today's visitor was particularly graceful and fierce, with a distinctive owl-like facial disk, dark brown feather streaks down her breast and belly, and glaring yellow eyes. When she finally grew tired of observing my quiet yard, she lifted off and flew—not *over* the trees, but *into* them—a deft and deadly navigator, a true wetland assassin.

It took almost five minutes, but eventually the smaller birds returned to feeding. The first ones back, along with the chickadees, were the daintiest and most widespread of our woodpeckers—the downy. Then another woodpecker, the much larger and more aggressive red-bellied woodpecker, came hurtling to land with a crash against the suet cage, frightening his smaller relatives away. This particular visitor was a male with a bristling red mohawk stripe. Red-bellied's are famous hoarders and their wild jabbing into the suet makes a small feast for the birds feeding on the ground below. Always eager for confrontation, scarcely any other birds can drive them away from a meal before they're finished. They stand about ten inches tall. While they love and depend on the suet in the winter, in warmer months they will visit less frequently, feasting instead on insects and toads and frogs.

GHOST SHIP / WHITE-TAILED DEER

FEBRUARY 19

Daybreak was overcast and fresh snow, not very much, had fallen. My grandfather would've called it a lackluster dusting. It seems our only bridge to the mainland has been damaged. Some mystery freighter, with neither direction nor crew, somehow jostled along the ice floes of Lake Bessie, propelled by the suction of a recent thaw and smashed into our bridge sometime after midnight. The sound woke me up—a deep, resonating thud followed by horrible screeching and cracking. That's where it sits now, lodged and ice-encrusted. Maybe it is a ghost ship. Maybe a torrent of spirits gushed off the tilted and submerged wreck to further haunt this place.

Seems plausible if you step outside today because the chill air carries the glum feel of caskets and requiems, of blue-skinned cadavers and gentle sobbing. Just stepping out there for a moment caused a wave of funereal nausea. There seemed to be a gentle but pained moaning coming from everywhere and the overcast sky above churned in blurry shades of tombstone granite, burrowing a blue hole of fatigue right through me. A good day to stay inside. At least I had visitors. Deer visitors.

Spent most of the day just sitting in that chair by the big picture window again, the Lady Grimalkin purring at my side. It was early afternoon when the white-tailed deer started to arrive in the yard. These ungulates are the largest mammal on the island and everyone knows there are too damn many of them, but they are beautiful and graceful. My admiration of deer, in my current worn-down condition, is mostly spoiled by envy. They are so nimble. They are also cautious, relying mainly on their sense of smell to detect danger. The deer wandering through my yard aren't nervous. They are shockingly at ease. A well-worn path of their making, never more evident than in these snow-covered winter months, snakes through the yard. Deer tend to use the same pathways for foraging which, once established, are hard to disrupt. Ungulates have hooves instead of nails or claws. You probably know these things. The first time I ever examined the hooves of a deer, dead of course, it was surprising to find them so thick and unyielding. Springy cork, considering their ability to bound and leap, had been my expectation. Between these hooves the white-tailed deer possess scent glands used to mark the bark of trees. These markings are messages beyond our comprehension, left behind for other deer and none of our business.

White-tailed deer will stand in one place, chew some fresh meal, then swallow with a big throat bulge and bring that food back up as if to vomit, only to chew and swallow again. It is because they have a four-chambered stomach glistening with legions of microorganisms who help with, but do not initially complete, digestion, and it is this partially digested cud that comes back up to be gnawed with that bovine sideways chew. Today I watched a pregnant doe emerge from the trees slowly, chewing like this. She was alone and graceful and her coat glistened faintly with ice. Easy math placed her at three months pregnant. Exactly halfway to giving birth. She had been eating for two—roaming the white landscape, browsing on twigs and buds and beneath feeders. I watched her approaching my feeders, but my moment of cozy wonder was disrupted by a disconcerting chest flitter.

My heart deviated from its normal rhythm.

A muscular scorch spread.

Cardiac distress.

The Lady Grimalkin seemed to sense it, too, because her head shot up from her purring repose and she meowed despairingly. This is it, I thought, my final moments. This window seat. This pregnant doe delicately making her way across the snow toward me, coming to nibble on fallen birdseed. This overcast winter. My breath came out in short gasps and big tears fell. The Lady Grimalkin would be left alone in a sad house with an increasingly foul litter box and no food and water and my corpse slumped in this chair. I closed my eyes and tried my best to breathe, to calm myself. And I did breathe. I did calm myself. But not before there were flashes of ambulance lights and the tunnel vision gasping in the red panic of those unwelcome flashes followed by narcotic retreat in emergency rooms and ventilators. All to keep my heart pumping, my increasingly lamentable heart. That last stay was the one I never fully recovered from. Too many tubes and too damn weak to get out of bed and actually look down from five stories up, I missed the big chunks of ice parading along in the blue lights of the shoreline. I just stayed there on my back, tubes in my nose in the dark silence, amid the calm respiration of the oxygen machine and the beauty of the falling snow. That last goddamn stay was when I truly became an old man. A man whose pace had irrevocably slowed. A winded and crestfallen old fool just one slip and fall from never sleeping under his own roof again.

When I reopened my eyes the concerned doe was right outside the window, wet-nostril breath steaming the glass. I smiled. Not today. Soon, but not today. The cat settled, furry chin resting on her politely folded paws, and exhaled a long, relieved sigh.

LISTENING TO THE MELANCHOLY ADIEUX

MARCH 3

The end of winter arrived with several days of rain that melted all but the most stubborn patches of snow. This melting, combined with the dripping of ice, has resulted in great rolling fogbanks. Today they were thicker than ever—a featureless, gauzy gray cloud that enveloped the house. The fog felt heavy and threatening and made me think of that damn ghost ship probably still leaned against the bridge. I gazed out and imagined wraiths. I gazed out and imagined the uncanny. Then something was seen reaching for me. Something clammy and awful and reaching to touch. Thankfully an unseen disturbance momentarily shifted the murk to reveal nothing more than the familiar black branches of the wild crabapple—gnarled, for sure, suggestive of tormented grasping, yes—but crabapple branches nonetheless. The damn fog caused other deceptions—two figures with skull faces and cigarettes that turned out to be nothing more than vapor and spruce. What I feared to be the pale collapse of a naked corpse in the flowerless wildflower garden was only one of those stubborn clumps of snow, and figures in ceremonial robes moving in a grim procession along the edge of the woods swirled off into the contours of tree trunks. Foggy deceptions, one and all.

The never-lifting fog inspired fearful possibilities. Suppose, I thought, a blue hand suddenly pressed into the window, bony arm stretching into the soup. Suppose that death hand pressed into the window glass until it cracked, allowing the fog to pour into the house? Or suppose a deer, spooked by the haunted atmosphere, came hurtling through the picture window? Suppose disaster, supernatural or not, breached the fortress of my tomb? These were my concerns, but nothing of the sort happened. It still made for an uneasy day.

While washing dishes earlier, a melody came to me. I started humming and soon my old, hoarse pipes were doing their best to sing. Hard to remember the last time music was played in the house. I sang some more, the lyrics streaming out of me—a song by the Melancholy Adieux.

You can never be quite sure what creates that shape
under the blanket,
although a carnation bloom offers a clue.
You can never be quite sure what creates that shape
under the blanket.
Tonight I hope it's only you.

"The Shape Under the Blanket" is from their debut album

released during my senior year of high school. It might seem corny now, but that was my favorite band. Most of my friends preferred the dangerous sensuality of the very short-lived Lady Morticians, while a few others became absorbed in the droning mystic sludge of the more experimental Deep Sleepers. For me, the best darksome qualities of both those bands overlapped in the Melancholy Adieux. So, when the dishes were done, and with the house still enshrouded in oppressively quiet mist, I started thumbing my way through old records with the Lady Grimalkin clumsily twining around my ankles. The first album plucked free was their third release, *Wire and Iron Grave Guards*. I dropped the needle and after a brief silence the guitars leapt from the speakers, sending up puffs of collected exoskeletons and shaking the wood-paneled walls. That first track, an instrumental called "Clouds Rolling In," is a frantic roaring thumper. Big booms and snapping rim shots and cymbal crashes. It is the music of primal energies with no regard for human life. It is music for tumultuous weather. The perfect antidote to this foggy day.

Unfortunately, the Lady Grimalkin did not seem amused by my musical choice and left the room with a contemptuous flipping of her tail. She seemed to know these songs took my mind away from her and into fond memories forged long before we met. I let her go, kept the volume up, and took a seat.

The Melancholy Adieux was an intoxicated and dangerously unhinged quintet, but *Wire and Iron Grave Guards* sticks to shorter, tighter tunes. All but one of the seventeen tracks clocks in at under three minutes. Side A contains nine songs tightly sequenced and always played together live as an exhausting twenty-two-minute medley, ending with the frantic two-punch finale of "Her Widely Known Sexual Exploits" and "Bone-saw Blues." Such tight precision was the product of constant touring followed by six weeks in a smoky studio strewn with empty bottles and candles, reverb and grime. Theirs was music that could get you into trouble. Slightly misanthropic creative types from every generation seek out such a soundtrack, and the Melancholy Adieux had the good fortune to emerge when such offerings were scarce. They followed *Wire and Iron Grave Guards* with a grinding sixteen-month tour in support of it. Their popularity peaked. Those two years were the closest to fame the band would ever rise. Unfortunately, it was also the last studio recording featuring founder Madeline Paderewski. The band carried on for several more releases, but there was simply no replacing her. She was a classically trained pianist from Oxblood, to the north, not far from the sandier shores of Lake Beyond. A brilliant musician, Madeline played piano exclusively for the band until *Wire and Iron Grave Guards,* when the bench was abandoned for an entire suite of songs in which she played guitar. The results of her guitar playing were barely musical wails and screeches. It was up to the rest of the band to maintain the integrity of a song under so many folded layers of sustained racket.

Madeline Paderewski was in love back in those days. The lucky man was fellow bandmate Karl Lutcher, and the intensity of their adoration for each other is widely accepted as the energetic stimulus behind *Wire and Iron Grave Guards*. Madeline and Karl co-wrote every tune and claimed the endless slapping thuds of their energetic couplings informed the rhythm of the music. Bootleg recordings from her last tour have become classics of their own and endlessly compared and compiled—not for the always reliably consistent opening twenty minutes when that first side was played with Madeline on guitar, but for the increasingly bizarre sonic explorations that followed when she rested her guitar on a candlelit altar and returned to the piano, or sometimes dulcimer or harp, for the mostly drifting remainder of the set. The sound of the Melancholy Adieux in these recordings very much resembles the sound of an extended debauch inexorably winding down—the sound of a group of aging friends who are leaving and moving on. Madeline's piano improvisations on these bootlegs garner particular praise, although the recordings are infamously marred by the heckling of less civilized concertgoers. She would sometimes respond to these hostilities by drawing any established tempo even further back and into, on sporadic evenings, long stretches of painfully uncomfortable silence.

Every set ended with an upbeat farewell, though—a rendition of the raunchy sing-along anthem from side B called "Embrace These Changes." Young Madeline Paderewski slurred and drawled about being brave, twanging her way through mentions of falling leaves and caskets. Today there were old voices joining in during the chorus, an auditory hallucination so convincing it caused me to shuffle over to the speakers to see if the woofers were malfunctioning.

The voices were familiar.

Voices of companions lost long ago.

When the needle dramatically lifted at the end of side B, the silent fog still hovered against the windows—more intensely than before. There was also the sound of a mouse in the walls. Mating activity for the white-footed mouse predictably kicks in about this time every year. They are probably nesting in the attic again. Gestation lasts about three weeks and the average litter size is four. If there are three nesting couples up there now, there could be a dozen mice in my house before the end of the month. A concern for some other time.

The second album to hit the turntable today, aptly titled *The Confusing Return of the Melancholy Adieux*, was released five years after *Wire and Iron Grave Guards*—five years after the tragic and spectacular death of Madeline, who had been tripping wildly from a fatal concoction of opiates and hallucinogens before wandering in a long, ghost-white gown to the top floor of a Helsinki hotel and right off the roof into big swirls of blizzard snow—meeting her end with a skeleton-collapsing shatter and splat over twenty floors below. They were recording an album of instrumental Christmas music when it happened. The band was never the same. Darius Feldspur, greaseball guitarist, made an acrimonious departure after the Christmas album came out. Their direction had become too far afield and experimental for his liking. He plopped his hollow-body Gretsch into its tattered black case, told them to piss off, and started a solo career, sadly playing in bars of diminishing size until he died performing an impromptu set in a fried-chicken restaurant many years later.

His records are around here somewhere, mostly traditional honky tonk. Regardless, after his departure the band was down to the trio of Karl Lutcher and fellow founding members Roman Lipsky and Derek Bottoms. They made a commitment to wearing black suits, no matter what condition either they or the suits were in. Unfortunately, as a trio, they found too much space to get lost in, their diversions becoming increasingly cosmic and incoherent, sometimes slowing to a nodded-out crawl where each sound, each note, died agonizingly slowly. Seeking what they deemed an essential counterbalance to their brooding, masculine bottle-draining, they added two women to the group—Sara Bathory Evans on harp and harpsichord, and Belinda Cox on organ. Alexander Minx, a notorious junky who had played with the Deep Sleepers, also joined on violin. They contributed politely, sparsely, comfortable as sidekicks. Karl was the unquestioned heartsick impresario steering the band, positioned in full inebriated bereavement in the spotlight, head drooped and vacillating, sometimes drooling, his eyes rolled back, stomping his feet erratically and laughing.

EARLY SPRING INTERLUDE

MARCH 18

There is no more fog. There is definitely no more snow. Only an exposed and overcast world of dead grass, fallen branches, and puddles. Ugly and drab early springtime. The dignified, snowy winter is over. There will no longer be any sustained cold. Springtime means three months of moisture and mud. No more weeks below freezing, only days; eventually, only hours. Temperatures today soared into the fifties and this wet shifting of the seasons has the Lady Grimalkin walking around bothered. When the door to the sunporch was opened around noon she wandered out, greeted by a chorus of gloomy drips and splashes. She faltered, paw held aloft, and the enormity of the situation engulfed her. She directed her nose to the damp air, registering the tannin decay and the animal scat and sprays of the freshly revealed landscape. It is a complicated aroma and this sudden burst of olfactory information took considerable time to parse out. She padded restlessly from one end of the porch to the other, sniffing at the screens, all bristle-backed. When she arched herself and hissed toward the woods, I followed her stare but saw nothing. Still, the

Lady Grimalkin flattened her ears, slowly backing away. We both retreated inside. Something was out there.

THREE LAPSES IN THE MIDST OF GRIEVING

APRIL 6

Morning broke with the shivery approach of rain. Long moments of calm followed by a slowly insurgent wind, like the exhale of a great beast that pressed itself into the house and made the gutters nervously creak. Weather was coming. Frantic whistling came from a couple of red-winged blackbirds, presumably competing with one another at the expense of my quiet morning, that were in the forsythia right outside my bedroom window. Then another swell of wet wind, spitting this time, and the same creaking of gutters. Damn gutters. The one on the back of the garage is falling off, big nail unhinged and hanging. Another chore that should just be ignored at this point, but those old impulses to climb ladders and repair things are slow to go. Another more concerning problem was the overnight loss of power. It was in my pursuit of candles and matches, halfway down the hall, when I nearly tripped on her—the Lady Grimalkin. She was on the floor, glassy unblinking eyes dilated to infinity and locked with mine, teeth bared and one of her paws erect in frozen preparation for a strike never delivered. Evidence suggested she had been scared to death. Had seen something too horrifying to endure.

In the hallway.

I paused. What sounded like human whispering was coming from the bathroom—a hushed conversation with even a giggle or two. The wind outside was now mysteriously quiet. All that could be heard was my breathing and a drip of water. Then more echoes of a distant conversation, coming from the living room this time. Two female voices washed away when the wind returned with a more sustained rattling, and sprays of rain pelted the windows. The voices had moved on and there I was—a bent and demented codger, looking for candles in some cold, creaking, and wheezing empty house, all bathed in the unearthly dim of a grim, gray morning, and kneeling over a dead black cat. Of course, I cried. Of course, there were lapses into memory—fragmented bits of recollections patched together over decades but all related to death, all related to mourning, and each producing its own wave of sorrow. The maddening chirp of ventilators, glazed and helpless eyes, grim hallways of nursing homes, the saccharine music pumped into funeral home viewings, the taping of family photos to boards, all with one person in common, the one who would never smile at you again or grasp your hand. Then the cemetery visits to various graves, even in the rain and snow, on special days of remembrance. You were walking a bit hunched because you were thereafter insolvent—bearing destroyed by the new emptiness and ache in your chest, eyes all reddish and puffed from your sniffling breakdowns.

I picked up the Lady Grimalkin, so limp and light. All the life weight evaporated. All the breath.

"The proper thing to do is get you in the ground now. A proper burial, as soon as possible."

Her mouth gaped and the wind howling against the house seemed to be speaking for her. Now the gutters would have to wait just like breakfast would have to wait. So out I trudged in my rain gear, bent into the wind and dragging a shovel behind me, carcass of my companion wrapped in a winding sheet towel and shielded in the cradle of my arm. The skies churned, darkened with heavy moisture ready to fall. The bare branches of trees frenzied into convulsions. Took me twenty minutes of digging and another fifteen to cover it all up properly but, when done, it felt sufficient. It felt respectable. She was put to rest next to the oldest of the eastern redbuds, and in a matter of weeks her gravesite will be celebrated with hundreds of fallen pink petals.

During my thirty-five minutes of labor there was another lapse in the midst of grieving when one very particular memory overtook me. It happened when the Lady Grimalkin was four years old. She had zipped away from my wife in the animal hospital parking lot across the bridge and was gone for three days before eventually wending her way back to us. There was a miraculous wave of relief when she appeared in the yard, licking her paws extravagantly, right by that same eastern redbud.

Of course, it was an entirely different day and season and we were both much younger. The sun was shining brightly and it was steamy and there was much more life everywhere. As I approached my Lady Grimalkin the reason for her extravagant grooming became clear. She had been hunting. She was speckled in blood and licking it away, purring and satisfied. There was a pile of feathers that suggested a mourning dove had been her meal.

She had demonstrated that mysterious ability of a cat to find their way home. Some have apparently traveled hundreds of miles in this fashion. To me it indicates some kinship with the night sky because they cover the most ground under cover of darkness. Cats seem to be at the height of their powers when given shadows. Maybe the vibrissae—those delicate hairs that appear on a cat's cheeks and chin and just above the eyes—do more than detect the air stirred by tiny moving prey in darkness. Maybe they also serve as some kind of compass, tingling ever so slightly whenever the furry faces of their owners are turned homeward and maybe, just maybe, the Lady Grimalkin followed those tingles all the way back to the island—a journey that would have taken her across the treacherous bridge. Did she tiptoe that grated span in the dead of night? Did she pause to look down and raise her hackles at the moon reflected in the waves below? I would never know. Of course, it was of no concern *how* she made it back to the island. It was a miracle to have her home. My sweet Lady Grimalkin was taken inside.

The blood and filth of her escapades was wiped and brushed away. I made sure her bowls were full. She found a pillow in the guest room and slept there for quite some time—for so long, in fact, that I remember being worried about her, worried that her adventure in the wild and the hunting she was forced into had resulted in some fatal contamination. Maybe she had eaten some poisoned animal along the way. But it was only sleep. Cats are slumberous creatures, lying in repose an average of sixteen hours a day. This is the reason all dreamers envy felines. My cat could rest like no other. Then the memory faded and I found myself still in the blustery outside, standing over her fresh grave. My teeth were chattering. A cold rain started and slowly transitioned into heavy, wet snow—falling fast, but falling into still unfrozen puddles and dissolving. My right hand, the one that did most of the petting and scratching and holds this heavy pen, aches sadly.

NEST-BUILDING

APRIL 22

Mute swans are working on their crappy nests today. These large birds are nonnatives—brought over the ocean on purpose by men in top hats to be plopped in city-park ponds, in the hopes they would politely accept their new role as elegantly floating ornaments. Unfortunately, and not surprisingly, these wild animals did not stay confined to their manicured human-proscribed environments. One day they were no longer there. One day both carriage riders and ladies on leisurely parasol strolls were disappointed to find the carefully constructed ponds empty. The birds had sought out wilder landscapes where they battled native favorites, the common loon and trumpeter swan, among others, for resources. The rhythms of the seasons and the centuries had lulled these native birds into complacency and in this relaxed state they were no match for the vicious mute swans. When these invaders found the Island of Wendake they claimed several sections of shoreline as their own, even though these other birds had been building their nests here for thousands of years.

Beneath their regal carriage and sophistication, mute swans harbor a sadistic proclivity for bloody behavior. A mating pair will establish a significant territory, ranging as wide as five acres, which they fiercely defend. A wandering loon doesn't stand a chance. Especially if there is a nest.

To see mute swans in their better moments, necks meekly drooping in a lazy glide, it would be easy to imagine them returning to a throne of some sort when day is done, maybe an ornate construction of artfully arranged twigs all lined with impossibly soft, fluffy down and further adorned with strings of gifted pearls, held aloft on a perch. Some seat of royalty. Some seat of dominion and superiority looking out over the waves. Nothing could be further from the truth. Theirs is the most pedestrian of bird lodgings—the ground nest—and not just any ground nest, but the most rudimentary type imaginable. Not much more than a primitive heap of pilfered vegetation, with a raised concave for eggs in the center, on exposed open earth. A crappy nest.

It's a wonder they survive.

The swan pair complete their slipshod construction together because they have been doing it for a long time, and because it works for them. Their viciousness alone makes this irresponsible nest sufficient for a monthlong incubation period. Their eggs are large and flagrantly visible in a watery environment crawling with muskrats and raccoons, but rarely do they lose one. Nobody wants to fuck with these swans. Most of us wish they would just go away.

Thankfully, theirs is not the only nest being built on the island today. Great blue herons, for instance, are hard at work. Full-grown, they typically stand about four feet tall. Having one at your side would be intimidating, knowing its strike is fast enough to snag leaping frogs. You would be obliged to be mindful of that long, pointed yellow bill.

Chances are it would hardly move a fraction because all herons, including the mysterious bitterns, have the ability to stiffen and remain motionless—water gently lapping against spindly legs some foolhardy fish believe to be nothing more than sticks wedged in the muck. Observe their occasional listing tilt, those branch legs hinging back and forth to mimic the fluctuation of wetland grasses and cattails. Also observe their graceful necks which can turn serpentine by virtue of specialized vertebrae. The same necks that are tucked back over their shoulders in a coiled *S* shape when in flight—soundlessly sailing along on the slow-motion flaps of a six-foot wingspan.

Great blue herons live in treetop colonies where mating pairs construct their own platform nest. These rookeries are rarely silent because these birds irritably grumble at one another, each pair wishing that all the others would just shut the hell up. But they are stuck in that community and that is where they will rear their young. It is where they will teach them to grumble irritably. The nests themselves are made of sticks, affixed in the forks of topmost branches and resembling the unlit bonfires of pagan altars. Building these nests, one stick at a time, is what the herons are out there doing today. Entire colonies are under construction in the barren upper reaches of deciduous hardwood trees near the edge of the water.

And there are still other nests being worked on. It is almost certain, for another case in point, that eastern screech-owls are preparing a soft and secret location for their eggs. Nesting for these birds occurs in tree cavities—apparently with a preference for those previously excavated and inhabited by woodpeckers. Eastern screech owls do very little in the way of actual building. They just move into an abandoned woodpecker den in a hasty mood and lay their eggs directly on the bare wood of the nest-hole bottom (although eventually this bottom will be furred with the downy remains of prey consumed, and consequently be much more comfortable). Egg-laying always happens in the latter half of April, with an incubation period that stretches deep into May. The eastern screech owl is a smaller owl, standing only eight or nine inches tall when mature, but it's a vicious predator. They will take prey their own size and sometimes larger, including squirrels and young rabbits. Larger prey, or any prey that cannot be consumed in a single gulp, will be taken off to a moonlit roost and ripped to shreds. Once I trained a flashlight beam on just such a scene and the bloody face of the feeding bird caused the flashlight to shudder in my hands. Never can more than a month go by without that glistening red vision inserting itself into some random thought.

That vision, shot in a sickly blue light, accumulates horrific embellishments with each new recollection until the branches visible in the trembling flashlight circle near the butchery of the eastern screech owl are all dripping in gore, and then, when that unsteady circle trains upward, it catches the reflected eyes of a woodland hag crouched in the higher branches—hunched in animal skins, emanating menstrual heat.

Should be no surprise that these particular birds keep such company. For good reason, their midnight calls inspire dread. And, of course, most people never see them; most only hear them. Theirs is a song existing in two parts. One sounds like the ghost of a distant horse reared up and whinnying, while the other is a sustained one-pitch trill. Sometimes they will repeat one of these over and over until the other arrives unexpectedly. Shiver-inducing indeed. Theirs is the sound of the haunted woods.

But we are discussing nests, not calls, and one last nest must be mentioned. It is our only regional example of a pendulous nest. These unique constructions are artfully woven every springtime by the female northern oriole. She is a beautiful, soft yellow bird with grayish wings. Her male counterpart understandably draws the most attention with his pumpkin-orange underparts and glimmering black head and back, but these cosmetic distinctions prove to be his only creature advantage. The female is the truly gifted one. Dwellings she constructs are the easiest to identify when scanning the bare branches of taller trees in late autumn. They are impossible to mistake for anything else. If you are fortunate, you will gaze up, and there—dangling like a satchel dropped from a passing plane—the pendulous nest of the oriole hangs.

Height is important to these birds. Their preference is to be a good forty to fifty feet off the ground. Of secondary importance is some open space nearby. They like older riverside trees or quieter spots where meadows and fields meet woods. Anywhere that allows them to rocket off unhindered in spirited flight, looping in delightful pursuit of fruit and nectar and unwary invertebrates. I've observed the female zipping down to the ground where a careful selection of twigs and stems and creepers commences. Sometimes you can hear the male letting loose his distinctive and joyful *peter-peter-peter* song while the female works. To me it usually sounds like cheers, but there are times I've noticed the laboring lady bird shooting him irked sideways glances. These don't seem to curtail his exuberance. Then once she has found material to her liking, she rockets back up into the canopy and continues her unique masterpiece. The female oriole creates what is essentially a pouch, usually attached to the tree by three woven loops. Each nest is unique because its shape is determined by the configuration of the branches chosen.

FULL SPRING INTERLUDE

MAY 6

The white pine produces no flowers, but there are other trees on my property that do, the most proliferative being the redbuds. The hulking stump of their long-dead mother rests on the curving end of the pea gravel drive, and over the decades they have spread. The delicate flowers produced by the redbud this time every year are no bigger than a fingernail, have always reminded me of ballet slippers in motion, and appear in the thousands on mature trees. Earlier today I went out to where the oldest of those redbuds stands, to visit the grave of the Lady Grimalkin. I pulled a branch down to sniff and on that same branch landed a Henry's elfin butterfly, flourishing and flapping from flower to flower.

I froze.

They are very small—not much bigger than the diminutive buds they pursue—and with their brushed-brown coloration and furry appearance it would be easy to mistake them for a tiny moth, especially if encountered at dusk or dawn.

This morning's elfin even took a break from flower hopping to rest.

Eventually my arm flinched, the branch shifted, and off

she flew to some higher perch, some more stable resting place. The branch released was restored to its prior position with a cantering blur.

The wild crabapple, a mature tree in our backyard now over twenty feet tall, is also in peak bloom. The flowers of the redbud and the wild crabapple coincide for up to ten days—sometimes as early as the end of April after milder winters and sometimes, like this year, well into the month of May. Their overlapping bloom marks the height of springtime. The bulging reddish buds swell and expand, and then, once the first flower unfurls, explode rapidly along the branches like the hem of a gaudy wedding gown, favoring the sun. The scent of these white five-petaled flowers attracts bees and flies. Some darker and breezier hour, with rainfall imminent, there will be a mass exodus and even now, as the air stirs, a pocketful of these blossoms are setting sail, swirling off and away. Their flowers are particularly short-lived, usually fully open for less than ten days. Even the trees themselves never last long enough, rarely surviving more than fifty years. The one in my backyard has been there a good thirty. She was scrawny when we moved in, but is now in her prime. It's reasonable to think she will never again produce a harvest as ostentatious as the one she is displaying today. It's also reasonable to think that next year her trunk will get a bit more twisted and bulging, a trend that will continue until leaves no longer return to the branches at all and her twisted frame mutates from charming to just plain haunted. Even now, as the breeze picks up, another confetti toss of petals goes flying. Those discarded exquisites will be followed by small green apples which are astoundingly tart when ripe. To make them edible you have to put in the effort of cooking them, sweetening them with brown sugar and cinnamon and such. Not a bad treat if prepared correctly, but to me the fruits of the wild crabapple are best left for wildlife. Some cling to the branches well into winter.

THE OVERWHELMING COMMON LILAC

MAY 22

Now the bloom time of the common lilac has arrived. The one directly outside my office. Temperatures today mounted into the low seventies and all the windows are still open. The lilac smell has been pouring in all day. Fifteen feet tall and heartbreakingly beautiful, her fresh and deep pinkish perfume has been overwhelming. Eyelids flit like butterflies on a basking stone, and in the swoon that follows there is a pair of strong and weathered hands resting on my arm again. And there is the nape of her neck. The tangled and inky spill of her hair tied back in haste and collapsing. The perfume of this flowering shrub has been flooding the room for several sunny days and when you are breathing in that scent with your eyes closed, sometimes you fall, tugged backward into dream-infused remembrances. The intoxicating fragrance of the common lilac advances through the air with intertwining propensities—each in equal measure—for smiles and sighs and tears, and those not moved by her enticements harbor the dullest souls imaginable. Those folks aren't worth it.

"Your hours are more precious than that," she always told

me. "Spend your time with people who can savor the beauty in things."

The common lilac has been in this country since the arrival of our founding fathers. This makes her an emblem of conquest to some but, in a purely ecological sense, she has made a courteous assimilation into the landscape and is an incredibly well-behaved plant. With a stately gait, this lilac has staged a redolent advance westward in the last five centuries, making it to my cold-water island about three hundred years ago. The common lilac has even been here long enough to become favored by some of our wildlife, and frequently a northern cardinal or tufted titmouse can be seen hopping from branch to branch—not only birds, but insect flyers as well. Today, in fact, an eastern tiger swallowtail butterfly was flitting from one flower cluster to the next. Lilacs are irresistible.

The common lilac can also be found growing wild along crumbling fences where she spreads by virtue of horizontal roots and suckers, and one day there could be an impenetrable thicket around this office of mine. One day there may be holes where the raccoons can come and go as they please. One day I will be gone and entire walls might be missing or, at best, leaning precariously. At that time the lilac thicket will methodically claim dominion and, with her prodding and wet weather progress, eventually bring the roof down—her branches and precipitation of all varieties achieving their patient demolition in unison, in harmony. For now, there is this single specimen outside my window, and although clearly still a shrub, in the decades ahead she will slowly assume the character of a small tree. Tonight she bears her lavender blossoms in large, running droops. My plan is to cut a few of these and bring them in for bedtime. At least enough for a bedside vaseful. Enough lilacs to take me back to bridges over slow-moving rivers in the midnight hour, a nip in the air contested by the afternoon warmth of tea kettles and cigarettes. Enough to infuse the perfume she wore to the symphony—a French program with works by Debussy and Ravel—a kiss in the dimly lit stairwell to the balcony during a more raucous section of *La Mer*. Then a long wait for a cab on the rain-smeared streets of Riverbend after the performance, the well-appointed crowd pouring around us. The common lilac hails from a cross-wielding and superstitious mountainous region, an ancient land of blood and bats and bones, accordions and hanging sausage, well-hipped women all ruddy and panting and irresistible—hands on healthy hips, smirking. And did you know her scent can also be infused directly into white sugar? My wife had several clandestine recipes for lilac-flavored treats. She kept them written down in one of her spiral-bound cookbooks where she left suggestive doodles in deep blue ink along the margins. Flowers much too vaginal alongside phallic elements extending their way to the nectar within. Recipes much too scandalous to share with the neighbors. These were exclusive. These were ours.

It is not only the exclusive consumption. The creation of them also belonged to us. She allowed me to watch and pitch in as instructed. The kitchen windows were open. There was always a house wren singing his same tune over and over.

She knew exactly when to cut the stems and bring them inside, as sure as she knew to smash the ends with a hammer and boil them to prolong their posture in a vase.

The common lilac is an effective and inspiring teacher.

Her flowers are also edible.

AND THE NORTHERN BOGFLUTTER

MAY 30

This morning was warm and damp and the backyard, with its high grasses and standing water, has resumed wet meadow status. The red-winged blackbirds seem particularly happy about this. As I watched a pair darting about, a flash of orange caught my eye. Something new blooming in the saturated green—a flower of some sort. My first thought was hawkweed, but it was too early in the season. My second and third guesses were also out of season. I pulled on some rubber boots and investigated. The plant itself stands just under three feet tall and has a flat cluster of orange composite flowers. The center-disk flowers are more reddish orange than the ray flowers. I squinted and shook my head. Even now, since consulting field guides and wracking my brain, I have no idea what that plant might be.

This, however, was the much less consequential of two plant discoveries made this morning. After inspecting those orange flowers, I went sloshing into the wet woods, drawn by the promise of finding more. Less than a quarter mile in, my shocking reward was a northern bogflutter in bloom. This was shocking for several reasons. First of all, it is a triennial, meaning it takes three years to reach maturity. The conspicuous red flower on this plant meant it had already been here two years. It wasn't the only one out there, either. It was part of a growing colony with over a dozen fiddlehead nubs just pushing up. Hard for me to understand how these went undetected. In its first year the northern bogflutter is only a weedy clump of prickly leaves you would hardly notice if not for the faint garbage smell, but in the second year it expands into a sticky ball and emits the terrible aroma of a rotting corpse. This attracts insect scavengers who become trapped and digested in the entanglement of low leaves. The plant found today was in its fruitful third year and producing the first of its two blooms. (The second, even more desirable, opens bone-white at the base of the plant in October.) In the third year it also produces fruit twice, then dies.

Northern bogflutter has a reputation for being a stealthy and sudden early-summer riser—leaves, stems, and flowers arriving fully formed in a matter of days. Adding to this illusion is their preference for places prone to seasonal flooding, far from any road, the more inaccessible the better. In these remote locations they will drive down a deep and bulging taproot, and emerge aboveground on a stage of sphagnum moss usually clustered next to, and consequently sheltered by, the shrubby bog rosemary. Bog rosemary appears to be a companion plant of sorts. There is absolutely no bog rosemary on my property, at least not yet. My property is swampy for sure, and a *touch* acidic, but nothing like the nutrient-rich peatlands of our bogs and muskegs to the north where bogflutter is usually found. Must have been a sudden increase in the level of acidity in the soil back there that was enough to awaken some long dormant specimen. The leaves of the bogflutter, stimulated by my presence, quivered with rapid excitement under more intimate examination.

"I'm poisonous," she called out.

"Believe me, I know," was my response.

There can be no mistaking this bogflutter. For starters, there are those stems—those wonderful and ghastly stems wearing a layer of dead insects, some still twitching. This freshly emerged specimen only had a couple errant ground beetles and a damselfly in her collection thus far, all of which were moving slowly, hopelessly.

And there is that singular early-summer bloom, so different from the fall bloom—a solitary blood-red bellflower the size of a large trillium. Another legend warns that gazing too long into such a bloom can drive you crazy. Seems plausible. The gory display is darker than, but similar to, the blossoming of the pitcher plant, and, also similar to the pitcher plant, bogflutters are carnivorous. The insects trapped to their stems with a sappy secretion are deprived of nutrients until only husks remain. The aftermath of bogflutter feasting can be found just inches below the seductive flower, on swollen stems adorned with prey. Perilous properties also exist in the leaves, which are similar to the fronds found on woodland ferns, and even in the bloom itself. Consumption is not recommended for an unprepared mind. Known as the mystic's companion to the north woods, northern bogflutter can be a slightly toxic and somewhat foul-tasting portal to the cosmic elsewhere. The term itself seems to originate from an unknowable bastardization of the Native American name of an interior lake within a pitted outwash moraine, alongside a kettle-depression bog, where legendary colonies of this plant once thrived. Wherever colonies are found, the air can turn viscid and pulsating. This is the case around the aptly named Bogflutter Lake.

Most people only know about it because of the murders. The weapon of choice in the killings was a bow and arrow shot by an avenging native from the afterlife. So the popular theory goes. Unfortunately, the presence of bogflutter colonies nearby prompted many to draw a connection between the plant and the violence, and you can imagine the type of wetland-draining hysteria this resulted in. Thankfully the land was preserved and the bogflutter survived.

There are two other disparate species, a fish and a bird, also called a bogflutter and usually found in the same type of habitat. The northern bogflutter fish, suspended by a sluggish fluttering of primitive fins in the shallows, is a rarely seen warty blob of a creature. And the yellow-crested bogflutter, an energetic but secretive little bird, can be found building her tightly woven cup nests in young jack pines at upland sites and in stunted conifers when conditions are lower and wetter. The bird has no psychotropic properties but a drug is derived from the poisonous liver of the fish. The drugs from the plant and fish provide dramatically different chaperones into the psychedelic unknown. The narcotic from the fish delivers only a pitch-black dulling of the senses, a float down a moonless night river, while the hallucinogen from the plant can be intensely visual, cathartic, and transformative.

It was time for some careful harvesting. I ended up taking the flower and several leaves but none of the stem. Such careful pruning will not hurt the mature plant and will allow it to bloom again in the fall. Once safely home, my treasure was inexpertly processed in the kitchen, where the presence of the clippings alone resulted in phantom whispers in the air behind me. There was nothing threatening about these whispers. They sounded excited, exuberant, barely contained—voices from another dimension heralding my return after too many years away.

The two customary ways to partake in the wonders of bogflutter are to create a tea for sipping, or it can be simply dried and smoked. Ingesting the flower itself directly is a third option, but I'm no shaman. The white flowers produced in the fall are much more powerful than the milder springtime red. The average effects from either last from ten to fourteen hours. My preferred method is the more refined—making a pot of tea, steeped lightly with mint. Upon sipping down two cups, I poured a third and took it to my reading chair by the window. The feeders were curiously quiet and the slowly shifting tree shadows of sunset transfixed me. Beams of light took on a sparkling brilliance as they faded. Clouds of tiny fish flies twirled and dissipated. Night fell with a rapid hush and for some time there was only buoyant darkness. It's hard to determine how long this lasted, but it seemed to go on for quite some time before I realized the darkness was just the result of my damn eyes being closed. Once opened, the sunset had somehow reversed itself and a fresh dawn broke, revealing an altered landscape of absinthe green, deeper and richer and more like summer mornings to come. A fresh warm breeze was carrying the intermingled scents of a field of early summer wildflowers; I crossed this field, heading toward a forest. My legs pumped in the muscular manner of a much younger man, carrying me not through the bluestem, but over it—careening like a clubtail. With just such a lilting flight my altered body was elevated into the trees and pulled into something warmer. Spinning tunnels of birds. A northern red oak wrapped in waving cranberry ribbons, collapsing from some maypole-weaving weeks ago. The persuasive breeze that cradled me decided to gently set me down by this towering tree.

The cranberry ribbons hissed and vanished.

A soft pattering of light rain in the leaves misted down to the forest floor and I rose to brush myself off—scattering big powdery puffs here and there. My luminous hands grew younger and stronger and larger, filling with blood and new tissue and gnarling strong once more. I smiled. The great oak tree slowly began to rotate, pivoting on a century-deep tap-root to carousel the extensive skirt of its other roots under my feet. I had been swiveled to a new vantage point, one clearly intended by the tree. A cabin could be seen, set down a trail not far from me. That's where I headed. On either side of the path were flowers resembling bloodroot, gently opening and closing their blooms like anemones reacting to the wake of my passage. Everything became watery, treetops smearing into aquatic grasses. Above those grasses, moving from one ambush spot to another, a northern pike nearly twenty feet long soared. His long shadow rolled over me and I froze. Other monstrous fish appeared after the toothy pike. A school of yellow perch passed, several dozen. Their lower fins are usually dusted orange, but the perch above me this evening had lower fins that were alive with yellowish neon flashes. A female descended like a falling plane and deposited a gelatinous ribbon of boulder-sized eggs on the former treetops. The next fish to appear was a single eight-foot-long bluegill, the spines of her fins suddenly sword-like and menacing. Imagine the size of the skillet you would need.

I rubbed my eyes.

The watery illusion dispersed but the cabin was still

there, now much closer and with the front door suddenly open. Music was playing inside. A string quartet muffled by cobwebs, coming from an old radio unplugged in the corner. Unplugged but still glowing. The stern voice of a designated official penetrating the static, relating important nautical warnings. I walked over and turned it off.

In the new silence came another sound, hardly noticeable at first.

The voice of a woman.

The voice of a woman lightly singing to herself.

The darkened room smelled of recently snuffed-out flames. Water was dripping into my eyes from a massive fallen tree limb that had smashed through the roof. Must've been months ago. There was an overpowering damp and woodsy smell from all the late snow and early rain that ponded the floorboards. To the east stretched an open sky and the nearness of a giant moon. The usually darkened pockets of the deeper seas and craters were fuzzed with butane blue—a strange light, leaking in furry beads from crevices where it collected and fell like tears or rain from gutters. A chill gathered in the air. Another closing of the eyes and we were away again, leaving a silver trail in the downpour. Falling raindrops liquified me until nothing was left of my body and nothing was left of the lake and nothing was left of the world but a weary blackness. There was the faintest sound, lightly thumping from somewhere in the unknowable below—most likely my heart, or the ghost of my heart if this really was death. What a disappointment the afterlife would be if the curse was to float in emptiness, hearing the ghost of the heart that thumped you through a life filled with so much. But this was not death, not today. It was my real heart beating and the blood it was pumping through my body was coursing into arms and legs, and soon I found myself back in my chair by the window with a cold and empty cup of bogflutter tea on the table next to me.

I was younger.

Even younger than before. Outside the rain was over and a late afternoon sun shone through a world of dripping green. Good time to get some more tea. The steeping had continued in my absence and the result was considerably more pungent. More mint was added but the burgundy essence of the bogflutter had spread until it looked like suicide bathwater and there was no covering up that taste. There were dull firefly flashes as the tea cooled and thickened. The fragrance rose. Several more sips sent me on my way again. An effortless drop. The cup was at my lips once more. Another pair of eyes reflected there—dark, alluring eyes that closed under the twinkling weight of garishly applied mascara and puffed into nothingness.

And it is good to be in this darkened house with the landscape waking up outside. And it is good to have this tea and to see that old cuckoo clock on the wall marching in quiet rhythmic ticks toward midnight, and to be spilling these lines out when I should really be asleep and then wondering if maybe these lines are spilling out *in my sleep*.

Tomorrow morning might have some answers.

LEAVING THE TRUCK AT THE GAS STATION

JUNE 13

Time to be careful.

A supply of bogflutter is welcome and rejuvenating, but can leave me with my defenses down for too long. It can be easy to get carried away with a dream factory like that blooming nearby. It can consume you. Even more distasteful, it can provoke religious behavior—the visions being so glorious that strong urges to worship the plant emerge. The temptation to don a lichen-covered robe and leave offerings, the compulsion to sing hymns of devotion, chant, gibber, make an ass of yourself. It can happen quickly.

Definitely time to be careful.

Just last night found me checking on the bogflutter. My flashlight proved unnecessary because the rippling emerald embers of those plants could be seen all the way from the sunporch. My reading over the years has taken me through stacks of dirt-smeared and earmarked field guides, but to get the full botanical picture of the northern bogflutter, you have to dig into more adventurous treatments of our native flora. *The Hidden Life of the Inland Seas Visionary Landscape,* by Walter O'Malley, provides the best account of what I witnessed last night—instances of bogflutter bioluminescence. O'Malley's descriptions of the plants shimmering like the northern lights are accurate. He conjectures that this behavior happens for a couple reasons—recent harvesting or grazing of the plant that causes the wounded bits to shine (which would explain why my particular plant is doing this) or tumultuous weather on the way that will result in nearby human death. The latter echoes original native beliefs. O'Malley also acknowledges that this wildly erratic display may be nothing more than a way of signaling a warning to the foraging animals of the nocturnal bog to steer clear.

Summertime has arrived with a hush. Trains that used to wail all night long have fallen silent. Days have passed without hearing a train at all. There also haven't been any hundred-foot freighters booming their horns. The Great Unraveling is underway. That doesn't mean there's not work to be done. Finally fixed the gutter, finally scraped away a big section of roof moss in the shade of the white mulberry tree, weeded out the flower beds to give those old blooms a little more room to breathe, took care of that damn broken shutter, trimmed away some dead branches and limbs, fired up the chainsaw. Then grabbed my shotgun and took the truck, with all three of my gas cans, down to the station.

Nobody was around. There were vehicles, but none that were moving. All were apparently just left behind. Some just oddly parked on the shoulder like orphan boats washed ashore—beached, stranded, no longer seaworthy. One with suitcases in the backseat. One with a rear-passenger door flung open. One windowless and further into the roadside weeds. Three times I stopped, cut the engine, and strained my ears to listen, strained my eyes to look. Not much to see or hear beyond the birds, but every so often there were faint glimpses of evasive movements behind cloudy windows, a ruffle of greenery, a group of shadows responding to the light breeze. Not much more. The island is a sleepy place today. So sleepy that a carefree herd of fourteen deer blocked the road at less than half a mile to the gas station. They seemed groggy, confused. Maybe they had been chewing the cud of roadside grazing without interruption all day and were getting lackadaisical in the heat. Honked my horn once and they all looked over. Held the horn down awhile longer and, as a group, they seemed to remember they were deer with bounding hooves and off they bounded. The houses they retreated around looked as left behind as the vehicles. Lawns grown into swaying knee-high prairies, butterflies flitting happily along. Some windows cracked here and there. One front door missing.

The engine was puttering as it rolled into the gas station.

As expected, there was no one around.

Nothing but mayflies locked stupidly on every available surface. When I stepped down, my boot crackled into a thick patch. Can't ever remember seeing so many. Every summer there is a mating swarm that descends on the island, but numbers today were excessive. Short-lived adult mayflies were clinging everywhere, the faulty rudders of their primitive and transparent wings flipping back and forth. These insects are crude reminders of the very first winged insects. Mayflies look primitive. They don't live long enough to feed so they possess no functioning mouthparts. They emerge from their aquatic nymph state to fly off to a spot, like this gas station, where they will mate at dusk and die hours later. Mayflies are clumsy fliers and can easily be picked up by pinching their wings together, an irresistible urge for some children.

No one in the little store.

Doors all locked.

Pressed my face against the garage windows to find only a single vehicle inside—tipped up and angled into the wall. Shattered glass everywhere. Pumps were empty, too. Adding to my tension was an aerial episode occurring directly overhead—two tiny wrens angrily darting at and chasing away a hawk from some nearby nest. One of the wrens anticipated the direction of the hawk's evasive flight and sliced a sharp beak across the neck of the offending raptor—the result being a flash of red and the hawk dropping sideways, still flapping wings but spouting blood and losing altitude. The wrens followed the fatally wounded bird all the way down to the ground, viciously striking and pecking and tearing out feathers. The three birds fell behind some willows in the direction of the canal and were gone.

Just down the street from the gas station is the Winchester Bar.

The possibility of cold beer.

The long shot of someone inside with answers.

I stood there thinking about it, hands on my hips, looking from my dead truck to the bar and back again. Concluded, in the end, there was no reason to deny myself a drink or two before the long walk home, so I retrieved the shotgun from the passenger seat, made sure both barrels were loaded, stuffed a few shells in the ass pocket of my jeans and headed across the silent street. The bar sign was not lit up. The front door was locked and the windows were too bleary to see through. Cautiously made my way around to the rear entrance where the workers usually took their smoke breaks. No one was taking a break today. No one working. No one around. Put a shoulder into the door and with a wrenching creak it opened. There was movement inside, something scurrying across the floor, and with the shotgun barrel leading the way, I eased into the darkness.

Someone cleared his throat from the darkened bar. "Hello?"

The voice was familiar, but I didn't answer right away.

"Who's there? Bar's closed," the voice slurred. My eyes adjusted to the murk and the figure on the barstool slowly came into view—a lumpish body sliding sideways as it awkwardly rotated around to greet me. I recognized the drawn and booze-droopy features. I put the gun to my shoulder and trained the barrel at his upper body.

"The hell you think you're doin' with that gun?"

"Mostly trying to keep the barrel steady."

"What for? Who cares?"

I let the gun fall slowly to my side. "What the fuck happened around here?"

The man shrugged. "Can't say. Wild turkeys are back, though."

I nodded. "What are you drinking?"

"Dust," he smiled.

"No, really. What are you drinking?"

He responded by lifting his glass in a toast. The motion elevated a glittering, lackadaisical cloud of motes upward, forming shapes that bulged in bluish incandescence until, one by one, they winked out. Then the man himself winked and slowly dwindled away. The empty barstool he left behind—now impossibly grim and awful—made me change my mind about getting a drink. Instead I walked home. A variety of willow trees, mostly poplar and cottonwood, have been releasing their fluffy, sailing seeds for a good ten days now. They were drifting down all around me—rising on the slightest updraft, changing direction like will-o'-the-wisps, and bunching in white clumps against benches and posts.

END OF DROUGHT ISLAND READING

JUNE 25

The rain falling today ends our little drought. Just when the exposed earth was parched and crumbling, grasses yellowing, dirt paths puffing with each footfall, water levels dropping, everything shrinking back and wilting—the rain finally poured down. Just when you've reached your limit of sun-bright ninety-degree days without a drop—whorish summer sun ascending, all engorged and reddish. Just as hope gets shrugged off and abandoned, the rain finally poured down.

It happened after the humidity turned unbearable and towering walls of clouds formed, sculpted upwards by powerful wind currents. By late afternoon these billowing embankments darkened and flashed lightning and the storms came marching in. Increasing tremors of approaching thunder were quickly followed by a frenzy of windblown leaves. The thirteenth lightning strike slammed into what sounded like a very large tree just down the road and for the next two hours the landscape got throttled. As much as the rain was needed, the intensity of it all resulted in quite a bit of unwelcome damage—a mess of snapped branches and dashed birds' nests, shingles pried from rooftops by straight-line winds, glass crunched beneath an assault of hail, and a towering basswood, about twenty feet into the woods, partially uprooted and left leaning askew. Other parts of the island must have their share of downed trees, but no chainsaws could be heard whining away when the storm moved out. Instead, when it was over, the dripping world got quieter. Thunder receded eastward. The air suddenly flushed clean and cool.

Today's reading found me back with my old copy of *The Supernatural Guide to the Twenty-One Islands of the River of Discards*. Found the bookmark placed in the pages back in frozen February and continued where I'd left off—chapter sixteen, "Lakeview Island." One of the lengthiest chapters, it tells the story of what happened on Lakeview in the summer of 1905—the year the Lakeview Island Company was formed. It was, for the longer part of history, just an uninhabited scenic outpost but once houses started to be built on the Island of Wendake, residents sought a nearby escape and cast their eyes to Lakeview. Here they could refresh themselves in the summer months—cooking the catch of the day and passing a bottle around, ships gliding soundlessly past in the watery darkness, the great silence of the placid sea and the open night sky. But things change. Soon families from outside Wendake discovered the charms of Lakeview—families mainly from crowded Riverbend looking for a breezy escape with picturesque views. They began boating down the river and renting spots along the water in the latter half of the nineteenth century. They pitched tents and assembled their own campfires. Some of these families were allowed to build cottages on their favorite camping spots in the 1890s, and these turned into the first permanent settlements. Lakeview promptly became and remains the southernmost inhabited island in our watery township. These initial structures were modest but photographs suggest they were sturdy and comfortable. Unfortunately, none survive. Now Lakeview Island is a gated community with one costive road looping past big houses, nearly all of them with their own boathouses and docks. The original pavilion from those cottage days still stands but nothing else remains. The pavilion, in spite of all the events held there, harbors no ghosts. In fact, not a single structure on Lakeview, according to Rebecca Livingstone, is haunted. But there remain the singular accounts of uncanny occurrences during the summer of 1905. The phenomena always happened during the working week when the men were at work and the women were left alone with the woods and the waves and the children. Rebecca recorded a firsthand account of events from one of the survivors just before she died. She writes:

> *Her caretaker permitted my entrance, and at her bedside I scribbled my notes in a determined effort to capture every fading remembrance, and, because my interview*

was decades after the event, it stands to reason all the precious details are also preciously faded.

That caveat aside, this account is convincing and claims the catalyst event happened toward the end of June—with a beach towel flapping on a clothesline.

Breezes off Lake Bessie were strong that day, the waves frothing into whitecaps, so it made sense to see this beach towel flapping vigorously to clothespin-snapping freedom, but it was the manner in which it did so that made the happening so extraordinary. The anonymous teller claims she watched the beach towel rise with intent and then spin in a looping spiral that was much too precise to have been guided by fitful sea breezes. This towel was, in fact, performing some of its acrobatics *against* the wind and nearly all the unexplainable episodes afterwards had something to do with objects levitating. What began with a mere towel progressed to items much more preposterous in size and weight. This inventory of floating objects experienced on Lakeview Island in the summer of 1905, from light to heavy and in order of appearance, deserves repeating—an accordion fan fluttered from the sand during one sundown, with children still splashing in the waves (an oblivious, large steamer passing by in the distance); a brass powder case shimmying from a vanity to fly out an open window (hinges working like a frantic clam in retreat); a flying fishing knife (easily the most dangerous of all the objects) that escaped a woman splitting walleye into fillets; a baseball bat that circled up in a dust storm from the on-deck circle and danced in the air for three minutes like the winged samara of a maple tree; and, at long last, a cracked vanity mirror set outside one of the cabins in superstitious aversion that skidded across the sandy ground for thirty feet before sailing out of sight toward foreign shores. These unexplained levitations had run their course by September, never to happen again. Unless, of course, the members of the Lakeview Island Club have been keeping secrets all these years. Maybe they gated the community to keep their levitations private. Not a terrible cloister with the blue vista of the open waters, the warm weather nautical adventures, the camaraderie. Maybe something is inexplicably floating down there right now.

One account of a ghost seen by a resident of Lakeview does exist, attributed to a man described as being *in the drunken haze of a costly divorce, but nonetheless reliable yacht club material*. It happened in the dead of winter when the lake was locked in ice. The captain claims that, from the perch of his boat dock one subzero midnight, he looked out over the frozen expanse of the water and saw a blue flashing in the distance, coming across the tundra, coming toward him. It was the shortwave phantasm of three iceboating boys, adjusting their homemade sail to catch the arctic winds before vanishing in a cloud of moonlit steam.

I closed the book for a moment and rubbed the bridge of my nose. The sun was setting to a growing chorus of insects in the darkening woods. When I resumed reading it was the very last chapter, and the briefest—chapter twenty-two, "Sturgeon Bar."

Sturgeon Bar is the southernmost island in the straits, a slender nine-acre strip of land surrounded by marshy shallows and shaped like the upper half of an emaciated duck. *Here is where the straits die and the sea is truly born,* Rebecca wrote. In her estimation it was a place that had always struck her as sickly and exhausted. She regarded it as the oldest of all the islands in spirit and reckoned it a location on the wane, too worn out for sustained hauntings. There was something undeniably shy and lonesome about Sturgeon Bar. It was a reluctant territory—a peninsula prematurely abandoned by the mainland and longing to either be connected again or, even better, just mercifully concealed by the waves forevermore. Sturgeon Bar, according to Rebecca, was essentially a place that didn't want to be there. It longed to be carried away. As for supernatural activity, legend said the bar could temporarily snag the restless dead who found a watery grave in coastal points north. She was convinced that departed spirits, having achieved an invisible state, were subject to the pull of the currents and almost never lingered at the spot where their heart ceased beating—not if it was near moving water. Those confused transients could rarely muster the energy for a defined manifestation and instead flickered weakly—a faint presence only detected by the most keenly adapted paranormal eye. Rebecca Livingstone, of course, claimed to have just such an eye, and recorded a handful of the sightings she experienced—most of them clustered toward the end of summer 1973. In what is the most unique stylistic departure in the entire book, she recorded her observations in verse, concluding the chapter as such:

and it was there along old sturgeon bar
that i finally saw the driver of a car
submerged upstream
a barrier-crashing suicide
stunned and smiling
in the fading light of lost years
and the hue is unmistakable
the somber bruising of dusk
that greets me at home
in the fading light of lost years
is where all the wayward exist
and where all the wayward
truth be told
always longed to be

BLACK WALNUTS AND THEIR LONE IMPS

JULY 5

There is a black walnut behind the garage, clearly visible from my bedroom window. Because of her advanced age she has always seemed like the mother to younger walnuts around here. Unfortunately, this matriarch was struck by lightning twenty years ago—as her daughters watched—and subsequently entered a slow decline. On the day of that storm the dynamic between the black walnuts changed forever, with the elder transitioning from the protector to the one in need of protection. She is roughly 150 and lingers on, with a permanent scar where no bark grows running along her trunk all the way to the ground. The woodpeckers are paying more and more attention to her, aware of her plight and the fast-approaching outcome that will convert her into a nice spot for a cavity nest, and all of this seems to have saddened her children a great deal. They regard one another from across the rooftop. They see their own branches still expanding while the elder's no longer fully leaf out. I'll be long gone when she begins her transition into a hollowed-out home for critters, long gone when she becomes host to colonies of clicking and masticating insects. They will slowly bring her down to the soil, snapping off her remaining upper reaches and carrying her extensive root systems away. Her dead branches will crash down on the roof and there will be no one to clear them. At the very end of her life cycle, she will cease producing nuts and offer the shelter of her body instead. There is a crushing ache in the long and solemn farewell of trees because the roots are so firmly locked in place. The mysterious beauty of these walnuts in early summertime—thousands of compound leaves with threads of alternately attached mirror image leaflets trembling like ferns and drooping with the weight of freshly formed unripe fruit—has kept me begrudgingly fond of them. There were years early on when, as a gardener, I wasn't happy with the toxin they leaked into the ground. They do this to clear their shadow of competition. The toxin is called juglone—a dull and melancholy word—and it successfully withers away a long list of desirable plants. It is found in the leaves which turn yellow by the end of summer and lazily drop. It is also found in the slippery black nuts she lets fall from forty feet above to pop loudly on the roof in October—sometimes just as you are falling asleep or sometimes, pop, like poltergeist activity in the middle of the haunted night to wake you with a mind full of worries and dark thoughts. Juglone is also found all through their root systems. Generally, you can expect the radius of the canopy, expanded by another five to ten feet, to be tainted. All gardeners living alongside these trees learn that this radius of toxicity increases as the tree grows taller but thankfully some natives, ideal for shade gardens, have adapted to survive, including trilliums, trout lilies, jack-in-the-pulpits, wild geraniums, sweet joe-pye weeds, and spotted touch-me-nots.

The disturbance was initially a cautious scraping, an apprehensive testing. Something tentative, secretive. Maybe the stirrings of a mouse investigating a possible nesting place. Not so. Soon the scraping intensified and was joined by the snapping of branchlets. It was coming from the older-mother black walnut. Beneath her there now lies a waving skirt of tufted sedge all teeming with insect life. It is a good place to go with a magnifying glass. The fallen branches tossed into the tall grass-like greenery beneath her have become the brackets for dozens of spiderwebs and that is precisely where the scraping could be heard—a determined scraping, escalating into an ill-tempered cracking.

Scrape-scrape-scrape-crack.

Some more rational portion of my mind decided it was a squirrel. It turned out to be something unexpected. Something I had read about, but never seen before. Something incredible. It was about the size of a small squirrel and a greenish combination of human and insect. It had no wings. This was a tree imp. His human face had a darkened and pointed chin that looked like a sculpted beard. He was dirt-smeared and about five inches tall. His compound eyes were the solid green of seedpods stripped of their husk. A mischievous imp—the type who resides in the hollow hills of the earth in hovels that smell of bracken fire and roasted shrew.

When the imp caught my stare he flashed a smile of pointed teeth which were still red from some recent carnivorous feast. He was navigating across the sedge—springing from tiny legs that were hinged and spurred like a grasshopper. These propelled him recklessly forward and each time he landed somewhere new he was forced to take a moment to compose himself. He looked directly back at me each time, maybe wondering if he was being hunted. I probably should have been in hunting mode. Instead I stood there as observer. He propelled himself to the base of the black walnut. An early evening breeze swept through. With one final leap, the imp landed on the reddish sundown bark of the tree. There was an inexplicable liquid ripple where his body impacted, then up the trunk he went in rapid ascent. There is a nest of eastern gray squirrels in that tree. They live in an old woodpecker hole, in which they had to gnaw the edges away to fit inside, and today it became the spot where they were cornered and killed. The mating squirrel pair built their nest and had a litter, born back in March. Thankfully the litter is off, old enough to collect their own damn nuts, and this mating pair were on their own. The imp seemed to know the squirrel couple would be sleeping and that was all the advantage he needed to scamper up the tree and kill them both. There was some pathetic squealing that suggested he was sadistically prolonging things and then the little monster emerged, blood-soaked and head-first. I saw him crawl back down the trunk, glistening with gore and carrying the trophies of his crime—two fluffy squirrel tails. He held them with selfish tightness and once again returned my curious stare with those beady green eyes. Then came the awful violin screeching of his laughter. I covered my ears as he plopped down into the tall grasses and escaped.

MIDSUMMER ISLAND REVERIE

JULY 16

Everything here has turned into a lethargic mist. Sticky with perspiration. Transformative summers of my youth were passed in old houses equally sticky—from the little blue house of my early childhood to a considerably more grimy and cluttered string of college-town rentals and beyond. Those summertimes—hazy to begin with and always getting hazier—were dependably backdropped by the unwavering nervous oscillations of indoor fans, curtains stirred by breezes that carried no relief, the dank smell of couches, the high whine of cicadas pouring unhindered into sluggish rooms on heat-wave afternoons, the sensation of melting, the salty taste of sweat combined with the childhood taste of lemonade, the young adulthood taste of alcohol and smoke, and the brine of temple worship. Old and familiar and nothing new.

It's important to get the windows open before the sun comes up, to let fresh air in. That's how my day started—a groggy room-to-room navigation of the house, turning latches and opening windows. The early morning air that rushed in was still cool from a night of open skies. Here and there, window by window, I pulled up blinds and paused a moment to look outside. The hoisting of the very first blind revealed a coyote in the yard, moving fast. She came sluicing through the shadows at a trot and then, sensing something ahead, sprang forth into a leaping sprint. The muscular power of that gaunt body loping away reminded me that these canines can run up to thirty-five miles an hour for short distances. Those oversized pointed ears. The sinister, narrow snout. The black-tipped wolfish tail. Coyotes used to get some people on this island in an uproar whenever some beloved smaller dog got carried away and torn apart, but they never bothered me. Ninety percent of their diet consists of mammals, like rodents and tiny dogs, but they are opportunistic and have been known to gobble down frogs and snakes. They are the only predator of our deer population but are limited in this capacity by an unwillingness to take on any animal larger than themselves. An adult deer will only be targeted if they succumb to illness or injury and when this occurs a grisly scene can unfold—the long muzzle of the coyote covered in blood, carnivore teeth pulling shreds of flesh and muscle away. Such a canine would probably be accompanied by his family and there is a good chance they would be joyously yipping while feasting. Coyotes, to their credit, form families instead of packs.

By the time I made it outside the sun was coming up bright orange through the leaves. A toad was behind the garage. She was backing into some loose mulch and exposed dirt, covering up for a long spell of heat-induced inactivity. She abruptly ceased her efforts in my presence and just sat there silently—forelegs flexed out in defiance, hind legs ready to propel. Toads are not built for escaping, so, for many predators, they are a plump and easy source of nutrition. For a lot of human youngsters, these amphibians are the first wild animals they ever capture and inspect. The kind-hearted majority of children always take special care not to crush or injure but, no matter how gentle the handling, a toad will always leave your fingers scented with its pungent toad stench. It is equipped with two prominent sacs, one directly behind each eye, filled with a smelly secretion which effectively curtails most examinations. It can also puff itself out and gush piss on you, because when you're so easy to catch you have to make yourself unappetizing somehow. Following these displays our local toad is harmless. Its call is a lyrical trill forever associated with the rainy evenings of springtime. The rest of the year it is almost entirely silent—austere and aloof and no longer interested in drawing attention—content to hop slowly and undetected beneath the ferns, consuming nearly every unfortunate insect in its path.

After lunch it was time to check on the northern bogflutters. They have entered another stage, having stopped blooming long ago, but their ever-unfolding leaves continue to provide both visual interest and psychotropic properties. No sense in letting them go to waste. Leaves are best harvested in the early evening when the heat of day has passed and shadows deepen, but, when the advancing heat and piling clouds indicated summer storms on the way, it was time to hustle out there for evening treats. I counted nineteen individual plants, every one of their carnivorous stems now blackened with a midsummer coat of dead and dying insects. Lean in close and you can hear the constant clicking and spasms of victims in distress—the nervous sound of an acidic massacre—of insects trapped and slowly being consumed. It cautions a harvester to tiptoe lightly, and today, during my nimble and hunched pruning, I had company—a pair of ruby-throated hummingbirds. They darted back and forth, rose in spirals and looped heart shapes through the air, meeting one another nearly beak to beak and then gliding backward in mirror images, the rapid blur of their wings producing a murmur—a display of impeccable precision and grace, and clearly some kind of courtship ritual. The ruby-throated hummingbird is our only bird that can fly backward. The throat of the male famously flashes from iridescent red to velvety black and back again and each specimen weighs only as much as a nickel. Pairs work together to build a cup nest the size of a monocle, using saliva and spider silk for adhesives. The little mating dance observed tonight above the bog-flutter came to a conclusion when they both blasted vertically, as if being sucked up some invisible tube. Near the treetops the male emitted one penultimate red flash from his amazing throat, and then they were gone.

It was time for me to go, too.

On my way back to the house something caught my attention—a sound. Another disturbance in the tall grass around the dying black walnut. Immediately I thought of the lone imp, and with a scamper and a hiss, there he was, reared up and snarling at me. I foolishly held my bucket of northern bog-flutter clippings up as if they would protect me, and the imp sneered at me some more, that awful fiddling chuckle, but this time his mirth was cut short by the sound of something else. A predator with the slippery movements of a snake, yet not a reptile at all. This new arrival was a member of the weasel family—an ermine. The fatal misfortune of the imp was that his fiddling chuckle had drawn the attention of this slippery brute. The ermine brought her snout to attention, sniffed her twitchy little nose, and honed in.

For something as small as the imp, getting targeted by an ermine was certain death. Recall this imp was only five inches tall while the ermine, a white-breasted female, was twice that size. Imagine an ermine twice your size. Those rounded furry ears and whiskers and the enthusiastic galloping gait might get them mistaken for adorable, but anyone who knows these murderous fiends can tell you the source of their enthusiasm is the chance for a bloody meal. This female had spotted the imp and with a despairing grimace he sprang away, but the ermine slithered in like mercury on a steep incline and was soon wrapped around him. With a splattering clench she was at least merciful and expedient in her killing, taking him with a bite to the back of the head and then, with leaping weasel undulations, eagerly lapping the greenish arterial fountain that sprang forth. The young ermine had been expanding her territorial boundaries, marking them with anal secretions, when she zeroed in on the recklessly exposed imp. "Never ever pass up an easy meal" is a motto shared by hoboes and weasels. Using her sharp teeth, she tore that diminutive prankster to shreds.

(*Almost midnight*) Just returned from a long walk—a good six miles taken at a leisurely pace—and found my house quietly humming and clicking. My hearing, like all of my senses, seems to be improving daily, constantly revealing new auditory worlds. Could be that gnawing has been going on for some time. Could be those tiny creatures have been gnawing away inside the walls for years. Regardless, tonight the infestation seems particularly loud and agitated. For a moment a portion of the wall flexed outward as if ready to burst. If that happened and a waterfall of hungry insects poured into my hallway, scattering to every unknowable nook and desperate cranny around the house, I'd be forced to find shelter elsewhere. My evening walk took me past one abandoned house after another. Some had broken windows and other breaches. Some were intact. Most, broken windows or not, were a lot nicer than mine. Sprawling three-thousand-square-foot ranches surrounded by trees, sitting empty. But my little place has all my books. It has all my music. Outside are all my plantings and trees and, with the neighbors absent, all the privacy I could hope for in my last year. I'd rather not move.

Some notes from my evening hike, while I'm still awake enough to write: I heard some strange splashing when walking over the canal bridge. The bridge itself, maybe because of the swampy heat, felt wobbly, unstable. The stagnant waters below were hard to make out—obscured by both light mist and nearly moonless darkness—but something was definitely alive and moving down there. The splashing was intermittent, half-hearted. Could've been a crayfish uprising. Could've been a black bullhead—a catfish remembered from the silty, brown creek behind my childhood home. A catfish remembered as being benthic and nocturnal and eager to voraciously gobble up anything that fit into its sloppy, gaping mouth, capable of stopping any crayfish uprising.

A fish remembered as a challenge to handle.

A fish ultimately remembered all trapped and downcast in the shallow confines of plastic buckets.

The splashing continued and sounded bigger.

Probably a snapping turtle—reptiles also remembered from the creek of my childhood, a reptile remembered as not to be messed with and heavy as an anvil. Encountering a snapper just emerged from the murky canal bottom wasn't entirely out of the question. I never saw what made the splashing. The mosquitos were getting pesky and I carried on, lathered in repellent but without a weapon, all the way to Firefly Drive. In my teenage years it was a favorite place to park a car on summer nights like this, long before any houses were built back there. It was just a densely forested dirt road where lots of bottomland trees canopied the path, an uninhabited stretch that reached the northern tip of the island. We never left our empties, but empties could always be found. The fireflies pulsed and lit up the woods in such astonishing numbers that you could kill the headlights and successfully stay on the road by aid of their bioluminescence if you drove slowly. Tonight it felt like that. I could almost hear that old Ford LTD crunching over the rocks and fallen branches, the radiant dips and smears of the fireflies forming an archway, a tunnel. Each species has its own unique pattern of flashes, but all are trying to woo one another. What we marvel at is their illuminated negotiations. Notice how many appear to be in pairs, every now and then joined by a third and then fifteen more, but always back to pairs, flashing urgently. Makes for a romantic setting, especially for teenagers with throbbing distractions in need of privacy. Sometimes there was a girl in that first car of mine. Sometimes there were wine coolers and cigarettes and condom troubles.

Both the adults and the larvae are predacious. They are also known as lightning bugs and their larval manifestations are called glow worms. The ability to locate glow worms along the ground, blinking in the leaf litter, is a proclivity one loses as the years pass and is always the strongest in children. Tonight on that dirt road there was more than the flashing ballet of the fireflies greeting me on every side. There was a midsummer insect symphony as well—the nervous chirping of the field crickets, the shearing buzzsaw drone of the dog-day cicadas by the hundreds, maybe thousands, the steady curtains of sound created by the rhythmic wing flexing of common katydids, and up above was a nearly full moon sending shafts of ghostly illumination through the canopy.

There was also a possum.

At first it seemed to be a large domestic feline in some sort of quavering and mangy decline, but no, this was a marsupial. There are probably still over fifty species of living possums and most of them are clustered in steamier climates of rain forest and jungle. We only have the one species on Wendake and this is about as far north as it dares venture. This possum is arguably the toughest of them all because no other can withstand the frigid winters on these northern bottomlands.

They don't even bother hibernating, prowling even on snowy winter nights—trotting with their prehensile tails stiffened behind them, the quivering embodiment of nervousness.

The one skittering toward me tonight on Firefly Drive had clearly been through her share of frostbitten winters. She was carrying her tiny pinkish babies in her belly pouch—each of them already immune to rattlesnake venom—and her ears were mostly eaten away from previous bouts of frostbite.

THE POISON IVY SWOON

AUGUST 3

Last night, maybe the night before, the screen from the dining room window went missing. Never could find it. It was my fault, but I decided to blame the raccoons. The result of never sealing up the breach was the skittering of claws on hardwood floors and a chattering yip from just down the hallway this morning.

I grabbed my revolver and went to investigate.

The old weapon is no longer stowed away. It's cleaned and loaded, resting on the nightstand after decades in a safe. Damn thing always made me nervous, especially once the aches and pains of advanced age kicked in. The sinister sidearm was always right there, waiting for the day when there was no sense in going on, when perseverance was no longer brave but foolish. Waiting for the bleak day when my mind was incontrovertibly made up. "Clean me every so often," it would whisper in its confinement, "so I'm ready when you are. Take me out and consider the possibilities." Every year I would give in. I would unlock the safe and take out that damn gun. And whenever I was alone the voice of the revolver grew more assertive, as if it had only been whispering to avoid my wife hearing. Once she was out of the house, especially in the months following the funeral, it turned strident and demanding. It was awful for awhile, but eventually calmed down.

Look at us now, me and my revolver—survivors. We've been reunited with no self-destructive intent. My protector is cleaned and loaded and nice to have around with the possibility of intruders and whatnot, but the moment I stepped into the hallway this morning, barrel leading the way, the disturbances trailed off as if being sucked into the clammy depths of a well. The following silence lasted for several minutes, until the bright, if repetitive, song of a house wren rang out from the great room.

Whatever had been scurrying around had departed, leaving behind a musky smell, commingled with urine. Something canine, maybe. Something carnivorous, for sure.

It was good to get outside. Midmorning was very peaceful. Not a single car or truck. No lawnmowers or distant shouting. Nothing but the symphony of insects, the chatter of birds, and the spreading heat. Beautiful day. I've had some weeds creep in where an old stand of wild bergamot has died out. It was hard to look at, so this morning I did some weeding. This morning those same old fingers were back at it, teasing invading roots free, uncovering worms, and tossing them off to curious nearby robins. Fingertips searching the densely populated subsoil, pulling up big chunks and massaging the dirt away. Sweating and maybe a little sore but whistling and smiling most of the time. Cracked nails and dirt-blackened hands are in my blood. Sometimes this results in hubris and a person should be extra alert when gardening barehanded, but today my lack of focus nearly caused me to grab the terminal leaves of a poison ivy vine.

I stopped.

What confirmed the identification beyond those three telltale leaflets were new berries the color of wet bone—oddly present on the main stem, weeks before their usual ripening in September. A trick of the shadows from the canopy above gave the impression these fruits were pulsating with inner light. I inched closer, plucked a cluster of five, and an instant warmth tingled my fingertips. Many birds are not bothered by the toxicity of these fruits but they can cause severe allergic reactions in mammals. Bringing them in for closer inspection, they twirled and playfully looped trails of redness in my palm. Curious, reckless, I scooped the toxic berries into my mouth and gulped them down like medicine. Their scorching descent left me stooped and gasping, eyes flooded and cheeks red, body convulsing to vomit but with the geyser staying dry. A burning sensation expanded outward from where they were being digested in my stomach, until it was too much to bear and I passed out.

Hard to say for how long I was unconscious, but when my

watery eyes opened again the day had advanced into a stormy afternoon. There were lots of bees and butterflies, drawn in by the powdery blonde sneezeweed petals, which were just beginning to open. Blooming sneezeweed signals the arrival of summer's concluding month. Even the leaves from the walnuts are turning yellow and dropping from their branches—gravity whip and gravity twirl to the withered grasses below.

Off to my right, a large buck moved through the shadows back in the trees, followed by a younger, scrawnier male. There were also three speckled fawns poking around the edge of the yard, browsing on lower branches but showing no interest in me or my garden.

Then, the sound of a voice.

Farther to the right, deeper in the woods.

"You need to come with us."

The utterance was muffled by the commotion of stormy breezes and roaring trees but those were definitely the words spoken. I rose to my feet and leaned forward, sky blackening above.

"You definitely need to come with us."

This time it was shouted and clearer than before, a different voice, not stronger, but closer. I looked over and saw the hot copper flash that comes from the tip of an inhaled cigarette.

"Hello?"

In response the sky opened with a violent spray of rain that sent me and my aching stomach scrambling for shelter—

but something extraordinary happened under the influence of those raindrops or, possibly, under the lingering influence of those poison-ivy toxins. Somehow I grew smaller and smaller as I splashed along until shelter in the wildflower garden found me diminished all the way down to tiny. I ran into the stems of a swamp milkweed as unyielding as an alder and the impact spun me down into the ground, sliding over fallen purple petals the size of dinner plates. There was an ominous presence of hulking milkweed bugs sheltered beneath the leaves above me. All of my wildflowers were over twice their normal height, some of them reaching nearly fifteen feet, and as the skies poured and thundered overhead the stems and leaves of those plants began to change colors. These alterations in hue happened in unison, beginning with sparkling green, shifting to golden, flashing neon marigold, and then, eventually, descending all the way down to a lewd burgundy, and in that bloated coloration, the fluids flowing through the stems were visible as gulping clouds of disturbance trailing in both directions. The rain continued, intensified, and crackling mortar thuds indicated the presence of hail large enough to decapitate me. So, in mud-splattered lunacy, I clawed and burrowed into the slurping muck, frantically pulling dirt away with both hands—*shelter, shelter, shelter*.

THE DAMN VINES

AUGUST 10

It's been a week since my poisoning.

Recklessly eating those berries resulted in three days of nausea, stomach sickness, and fever. It kept me inside, suffering through long stretches of unconsciousness, with occasional groggy awakenings to oppressive late-summer heat. Unfortunately, there were times during the first twenty-four hours when fits of nausea and stupor overlapped. The result made a real mess of the living room that I was too depleted to clean up. Even worse, these messes contained seeds that have festered into new vines—not exactly poison ivy, but something influenced by the bogflutter in my system and much worse. The damn vines, in only a matter of days, sprouted, climbed across the floor, and this morning were over three feet up the wall.

At first, I assumed small rodents or large insects were calling the freshly emerged vines home. There were movements. Sometimes a shudder that ran the length of a particular leafy strand, as if tickled by a breeze. Then I witnessed some creepers, in a wondrous fluctuating ascent, actually scaling the wall—a section of vine slowly extending a grasping tendril and unfurling a leaf in a matter of minutes. These vines had to go, or it was time for me to pack up and move. The enormity of the task, combined with the sleep-inducing presence of these plants, made me unbearably fatigued and slumber took me down, over and over. Upon waking, the vines would be that much further along—spreading, climbing. This was definitely something worse than poison ivy. Checking field guides was useless. This creeper, birthed of what my body expelled, was clearly something nonnative and invasive, and what further differentiates it from any vine, in my experience, is the ability to generate heat. In the darkest pitch of night the leaves can be seen glimmering faintly like legions of scattered distant furnaces—reddish with delicate combustion. Then there is the damn smell, which continued getting stronger, toxic hour by toxic hour.

Today was finally the day those vines were removed.

It wasn't easy.

Out in the garage were the essentials—gloves, face mask, plastic contractor bags, small rake. The heat was stifling today, but layers of protection were required, including a long-sleeved work shirt that had no holes, buttoned tightly at the wrist. It was sweaty work but most of it was done in under thirty minutes. Upon contact some vines changed to bloody red and emitted a vaporous puff. Felt lucky to have a good mask. Whatever substance they bled out when damaged had powerful properties, and my fingers and arms, protected as they were, started to tingle as those poisonous strands were yanked and stuffed away. A few became animated in their stunned outrage and wheeled around like drowsy vipers to strike at me, one even attempting to clasp my shirt and crawl up to my face. Thankfully their attacks were strangely languid and easy to fend off.

The vines climb by aerial roots and small adhesive disks; the circular remnants of those disks still need to be scrubbed away.

A MIGRATION OF SNAKES

AUGUST 26

The good news is my health has returned—not only recovered from my reckless self-poisoning and free from toxic vines, but stronger and better than ever. The bad news is that this rejuvenation was tested by the invasion of hundreds of snakes today. It reminded me of the old song "The Jungle" by Diablito, set to a melody by Grieg. Even at this late hour, the quell is disrupted by a slithering susurration of unknown origin. It's not easy to relax. It's been a long day of reptiles and steady precipitation. A long day of cautious hunting, punctuated by sudden bursts of predatory energy, of pinning and grasping and removing. Something uprooted most of the local snakes, and they were on the move. My definitive tally of slithering intruders today, ones that made it *into* the house, was nineteen. This means there are clearly some structural issues with this worn-out place. I understand. Those issues weren't getting fixed today, so the house remains unsettled. A lingering miasma of reptilian distress hangs in every room. It's an effective stimulant, more powerful than campfire coffee, and sleep won't claim my jittery ass anytime soon. Might as well write.

At least cooler night breezes are making their way through the open windows. Feels like it might even get down into the forties before dawn, which in turn might put any remaining snakes into a more dormant state. At the height of the activity, which coincided with a late afternoon downpour, there easily could have been over a hundred out there, all slipping southward as if fleeing a common and terrible enemy. They inevitably crossed paths with each other, followed by hissing and striking. Lots of garter snakes, primarily the butler's garter and the common garter. The day started, in fact, when I found what was either a butler's or a younger common garter in the bathtub. Both share the same coloration and lengthwise white stripes on their black-scale bodies and can easily be confused, but any specimen longer than two feet has to be the common garter. Unfortunately, the one in my tub this morning was just shy of two feet, and in a foul mood, too. I could smell it. I had handled plenty of garters growing up. They were easy to find along the railroad tracks that ran between my childhood house and the river. I'm sure there are still plenty over there now, probably more. I had lifted enough of them to know they almost always try to bite when first touched. Dodging that initial attack is usually all you have to do. Otherwise, they're relatively docile. These were the snakes that had gone wrapping and coiling first through my then-adolescent hands. Today one of those garters was in my bathtub and I wasn't happy to see it. He was in a hateful mood.

Better get some gloves.

I gently closed the bathroom door and sealed the bottom off with towels, then headed out to the garage. The sun was nearly up and a light island breeze was blowing, insects slowly winding down after a raucous evening. Something felt unnaturally humid and wrong about the day. There was movement on the driveway, not twenty feet away—a single and brightly colored milk snake close to three feet in length, winding in a determined fashion across the pea gravel. This female was wearing the garish red morph that gets her mistaken for venomous—splashed with bright saddle-shaped markings, each outlined in black on a white body. Famously secretive and rarely seen, she is a classic barn snake. What my grandmother called a woodpile creeper. The milk snake had moved on by the time I emerged from the garage, pulling on my gloves, but another snake had taken her place. Three snakes in one morning, following years of not seeing any at all. Something had them dislodged and on the run. Images of animals pouring in a panic away from a wildfire sprang to mind, but this was a soggier menace affecting only one kind of reptile, as far as I could tell.

Thankfully the garter was still in the tub when I returned.

He was promptly pinned and escorted outside, where slithering could be heard everywhere.

Hard not to think about a routinely dismissed, but now pretty damn compelling, old sailor's tale about the voyage of the *Windhover,* which sailed through this archipelago back in the summer of 1679. The *Windhover,* famous ghost ship of the inland seas region, was a fifty-foot barque with big, flapping sails, long loops of rigging, and an elegant glide. She carried the first Europeans up the River of Discards, and a priest aboard kept a journal. The priest was a mundane writer, but the most inspired section of his account recorded a satanic scene on what would later be called Wendake, eerily similar to what happened today. His report christened the location as Isle of Serpents, and this identification appeared on some eighteenth-century maps but was abandoned when early Christian settlers found the place with no more reptiles than any other. However, in the priest's account, there were snakes in such numbers that their accumulated slithering caused waves. These ripples advanced in rhythmic pulses, swaying the doomed ship eerily back and forth, and the missionary recorded the sound of whispering in the air, more like the brushing of reptile scutes than the uttering of humans. Voices emerged from this eerie chorus, voices he claimed could only have belonged to demons. It was his belief that unholy enchantments often disguise themselves in the sounds of nature, relying on familiar strains to cloak their hidden malice until the snares of their spells had been fastened tight and it was too goddamn late.

The priest on board the *Windhover* recorded that several bewitched sailors had to be pulled from the railing to prevent them from leaping overboard. Only diabolical forces could render men so witless. There were devils living on the Island of Wendake—the holy man was absolutely sure of it—and he pleaded with the captain not to linger and pick up speed if at all possible. The captain said of course, and off they sailed, the heavy darkness of the place subsiding with each mile traveled north. The *Windhover* unfortunately sank two weeks later in the depths of Lake Beyond.

By midmorning, when bad weather lit up the horizon and wind swept through the leaves, the invasion had officially begun. Nearly everywhere the ground was moving—grass, dead leaves, and fallen branches animated by hundreds of snakes. Lightning flashes revealed crawlers of various sizes, the smallest among them not much larger than worms but tapered and fast, unidentifiable. The black walnuts were furiously casting down yellow leaves as if to shoo them away, and it started raining hard—an instantaneous blinding downpour, a frenzied and inhospitable splashing that turned gutters into frothing rivulets, like phones ringing endlessly.

My obsessive reflections on what constitutes a snake only added to my unease. Its teeth, for instance. Not just the fangs, either. The massasauga rattlesnake is our only venomous snake, but it was conspicuously missing from today's slithering hordes. The most reckless way to tell if a snake is venomous or not is to look into its eyes. Nonvenomous snakes all have round, innocent pupils, while those packing poison all have elliptical cat eyes, and every snake, venomous or not, has those *other* teeth—teeth hooked backwards off unhinging jaws which are not meant for chewing at all, but instead have the sole purpose of holding prey in place. It takes time to swallow, one lugubrious gulp at a time. It takes time to subject victims to one of the most gruesome deaths in the animal kingdom. Imagine being eaten alive, going down the throat of a serpent, your knowing eyes wide with terror, your tufts of fur or feathers disappearing, and the gurgle of blood, the click of bones. And then you're gone into the darkness of the mouth and its searing pain of digestive juices. Your eyes are functioning quite well, but the sunlight is gone forever. No more colors to see, just the red insides of your killer.

This migration of snakes is a sign of much worse things to come.

END-OF-SUMMER INTERLUDE

SEPTEMBER 2

The landscape is still recovering and late afternoon advances at a crawl—gloomy and raw, ragged masses of purple clouds churning with no end in sight. Some of my flowers got trampled and destroyed by those marauding snakes. I'm particularly upset about the asters. Something about seeing those cracked and slimy stems, flowers unbloomed—shriveled, transpired—just broke me. Out poured the kind of anguished tears that have the ability, regardless of their immediate inspiration, to pry open that usually sealed-off well where memories of all the hardest weepings persist. You start crying about the death of a native perennial and end up remembering tears over a lost feline. And tears over a lost feline are invariably linked to other piteous breakdowns involving cats and lovers alike. If you cry long enough you can travel backwards in time, encountering one long-past source of dispirited nose-blowing after another until eventually, if remaining steadfastly linear, the weeper ends up remembering the searing pangs of the newborn hunger for milk.

I didn't cry that long today.

But I did cry long enough to go back decades. Providing

you with some random images certainly qualifies as another lapse in the midst of grieving, but without names attached they are harmless enough. For example, what could possibly be gleaned from an umbrella left upturned on a rainy sidewalk, pivoting gently back and forth like a carnival ride coming to rest? And tears. Or a lilac perfume splashed liberally behind an ear and a long farewell embrace? And tears. And the sputtering of flames and a fractured leg pinned awkwardly, holding a man in place who discerned, even through the blunted haze of a concussion, that there was no one else moving or even breathing in either the front or back seat. Just the fool with the keys. And tears. When done with my crying, I forced myself up. Since there didn't seem to be anyone in the neighborhood anymore and there was neither time nor energy for a longer walk, the idea was to aimlessly wander the neighborhood. Fresh air always helped. A good walk. Unfortunately my compass was kaput, and erosion of common sense guided me to a depressing spot—a miserable in-ground pool two streets down. I've wandered over there before. There is something wrong about that pit of rainwater and fallen leaves, but lately it transfixes me, pins me in contemplation for too long, just staring—that foul air of decay drifting up around me, almost visible, fetid and faintly yellow, a perfume of desecration in the dull heat of the late summer sun, a perfume of dead lily pads and muck, of drowned and decomposing snakes, of ghost slitherings and the echo of long-gone splashing. There might have been human bones in the cheerless shadows, revealed by breezes—flashes of skeletal white, a ribcage, the outlines of empty sockets, a hand with fingertips testing the rippling membrane above as if clawing at a coffin lid. This might be where I will come lie down—where I will curl up in surrender, coiled like a millipede, exoskeleton brittle and crackly and already collapsing inward. Then I look down into that pool again to see my reflection—glassy blue eyes unblinking in the moonlight, anguished lips pulled back to reveal discolored teeth and the movement of beetles.

THE HORROR OF THE CARRION HAWK

SEPTEMBER 13

The hawk migration hits full swing in mid-September, so this morning found me at the water's edge, gazing skyward. A light breeze was promoting corkscrews of thermal updraft and the river was getting choppy. Perfect conditions. The first hawks in sight were a few of the sharp-shinned variety, and they were riding these updrafts, never coming close to the ground, just soaring from one thermal column to the next, impatient to be off. Then, not far behind, came the first of the broad-winged hawks, curving along in a group of six. These two are very similar when seen from the ground, and the easiest way for a novice to tell the difference is by the tails. A sharp-shinned hawk has a narrow, pointed tail that resembles a large paintbrush, while that of the broad-winged is in the shape of a woman's fan splayed open. They are often seen together, but the sharp-shinned hawks are outnumbered. You always see more of the broad-wingeds. An impressive bird to observe, the broad-winged hawk prefers dense, wet forests—boreal in the summer and tropical in the winter. She is packed and muscular with short but expansive wings, and if you're lucky enough to see one perch for long enough, you will notice the rusty-brown barring of her chest feathers and how frequently she ruffles them in agitation. This is not the kind of bird that seems to relax much. Those wild, intense eyes, always scanning. No other migration along the River of Discards compares with the spectacle of their departure every fall, which numbers in the tens of thousands.

This morning there were hundreds of other hawks—their flight paths overlapping in a busy confusion that lasted hour after hour, intensifying as morning progressed. Shortly before noon the numbers fell off ominously and intuition told me it was time to go. Instead, I lingered and saw a monster. Until today, the only raptors documented on Wendake were the aforementioned two, along with the red-tailed hawk, the red-shouldered hawk, the osprey, the bald eagle, the American kestrel, the peregrine falcon, the Cooper's hawk, the rough-legged hawk, the northern goshawk, and the northern harrier.

An unlucky thirteenth can be added to the list.

One that is significantly larger than the rest.

For the sake of naming things, I'm calling this bird a carrion hawk and as soon as I sighted it through my binoculars—the immensity of it apparent as it aggressively collided with other birds—the horror sent me running for home, scurrying under the cover of tree canopies like a rodent. While making my retreat there were moments when the carrion hawk seemed to be upon me. A sudden breeze disrupting the leaves, and the passing shadow of a cloud, once sent me diving into some roadside brush that unfortunately contained thistle. The illusion passed and the monster bird could be heard, croaking an unpleasant call further off. It seemed I had successfully avoided detection when my little house came into view and I slipped inside. Then, a little over an hour ago, it found me.

I was working on a crude sketch of the creature (since crumpled off and discarded) when my pencil stopped.

Sounds outside.

At first a labored creaking of branches, some snapping.

I looked.

This bird, the carrion hawk, has an eight-foot wingspan and a head larger than my own. She is essentially an unwholesome combination of our largest hawks and a turkey vulture. The rusty-brown streaking in her feathers, and muscular stature, are very hawkish, but she is topped with a shocking, featherless red-and-black head, clearly adapted for rooting in carcasses. This was, however, no mere carrion scavenger ghoulishly waiting for the next body to drop. This was a predator with an empty stomach. Her hawkish tendencies were the giveaway—hungrily scanning the landscape, neck feathers puffed out in irritation. She was hunting.

Another striking characteristic of this bird is the gory coloration on both her flank and undertail. Hers was most certainly a nest filled with bones—many of them fractured by talons, crushed out of pure spite. An indiscriminate and heartless killer. Anthony Selfridge, in *The Bellsnickle and Other*

Legends of Lake Manitou, tells the campfire classic of large birds, probably very much like this carrion hawk, which had nesting sites on remote islands scattered not only around Lake Manitou, but in Lake Beyond as well. Much like the dreaded bellsnickle, these monster birds were known to carry off children, especially those who stayed up too late listening to campfire stories. Selfridge identifies two variations of the creature—the gunchy bird and the goony bird. The folktales about both are remarkably similar and characterized by violence. I carefully began inching away from the picture window and she caught my movement.

I froze.

The black pupil dilated in her tannish, animated eye as she sized me up, and then—with what sounded like a gurgling laugh of satisfaction and mockery—the carrion hawk flapped her great black wings and sailed off over the trees, with a gusty disruption of already yellow walnut leaves.

(*Later*) Her second visit was at sundown. Scared to leave the house, I hunkered inside as if in quarantine or under surveillance. Every window approached and passed with caution. More firearms would be nice. More than the shotgun and revolver, an *arsenal* would be nice. The old house seems a lot more vulnerable today. But maybe, just maybe, that monstrosity had been called onward by her appetites. Maybe her gurgling laugh was just saying, "A skinny little primate like you is not worth my goddamn time." Maybe she flew off in search of cows on mainland farms. Maybe this, instead of the rain, was what the snakes were fleeing. Maybe other even more fantastical creatures will be steering a path away from winter through the River of Discards this year. Maybe this carrion hawk was the first in what would become a parade of destructive oddities.

Sundown brought the promise of a respite because hawks are diurnal, but not so with this creature. Just as the sky was darkening, the sound of great flapping was heard again, circling above. I grabbed the revolver. Her great wingspan shadow fell across the yard and the house, and moments later she landed clumsily on the roof. The thump of impact shook dead flies from lampshades and rattled kitchen-counter plates. The beast could then be heard rumbling with guttural croaks and prying at some of the damaged shingles. Loud splintering followed, and a thumping that was clearly her leaping up and down in place, trying to bring down the structure beneath her. I got to my feet, gun raised and aimed at the ceiling. After several minutes of this the bird got either frustrated or bored. She could then be heard scrabbling aimlessly about, doing even more damage, but in a more random and distracted fashion. I kept quiet and still, trusty revolver clutched tightly, until something else caught the attention of the beast and she flew away, this time into the night. This was definitely the bird my grandmother warned me about on those summer vacations by the shores of Lake Beyond, campfire burning, and bony finger crooked to the sky in warning. This was the great bald-headed raptor with the savage eyes that was big enough to carry me off.

THE GLOOM COMES THROUGH

OCTOBER 1

The menacing hawk no longer menaces me, but she left my roof in bad shape. Just as the wind shifts and turns colder.

Time has come for me to find a new house. My attempt to do so today didn't get far because the weather took a rainy turn. It happened before I even made it to the end of the road, starting with some light sprays of wetness.

There was movement in nearby shrubs where a new shadow was emerging. Sleek and mysterious, it moved, a slippery and darker smudge, followed by a flash of green eyes and the flicking of a tail—a cat. Emerging from the same shadows, only moments later, was a woman who looked familiar—as if scrubbing away the grime and musk of a rugged outdoor lifestyle would reveal an old neighbor or teacher. It was the way she squinted that caught me right away. The wind shifted with a new pelting of rain, causing me to blink, and this was all it took to dispel my ghostly visitors. I went back inside.

The haunting season has arrived on the island.

THE GHOSTS

OCTOBER 22

The day began gloomy and cold, so I wore boots and a heavier jacket when going outside. It was time to check on the northern bogflutter. Looking over my shoulder with the telling frequency of a man expecting something to be there, and walking with bravado, I attempted to whistle. Anyone who has been haunted can sympathize. But there were no ghosts in the dark entranceway when I pulled my boots on, and there were no ghosts hiding in the overgrown path along the garage. Nor were there ghosts out by the northern bogflutter—just the plants themselves. My little patch is in a healthy state and blooming again. The trampling of those passing snakes had catastrophic potential but didn't cause any lasting damage. Their intertwining slithering seemed to act as a stimulant or fertilizer. They were blooming furiously, tiny white October flowers. These could be snipped neatly at the base of the clasping stem attachment and immediately dropped into a stoppered jar filled halfway with purified water. This cutting is preferably done at sundown with a pair of gardening shears that have never been used before. The flower, once snipped in this fashion, will retain its properties of enchantment for up to six hours.

My writing was interrupted.

Knock-knock.

The dreary morning was dripping from a passing shower.

Knock-knock-knock.

The empty doorstep could be seen through the barren lilac branches from the office window—no one was standing there.

Knock-knock-knock-knock!

Someone not suffering from ghosts would find it completely unnecessary to go answer a door where no one is knocking. A haunted person sees thing differently. As soon as I stood up, the knocking stopped, and, as I made my way slowly to the door, it began again. This time as a light, playful tapping, which descended into a scratching. It was coming from the bottom of the door and getting aggressive, causing damage to the wood. She was back. She has been coming around mostly in the evenings, making this morning visit a surprise, but I knew it was her. The scratching stopped after one long, gouging scrape and I opened the door. Looking up at me with her green eyes was my cat.

She's really not my cat anymore. She is gaunt and only comes here to nap in old, favorite spots. Once awake, she is quick to slip into hunter mode and be off.

Her lady companion, who has been here twice now, looks vaguely familiar and is an excellent storyteller—tall tales, ghost stories. Previous visits happened many napping hours after the arrival of the cat. This morning she was only a few minutes behind. She knocked and was raising her hand for another round of knockings, but I opened the door before her fist fell.

"Good morning."

She smiled at me, then looked down to where the Lady Grimalkin was pacing.

"My little furry friend. She smells like dead leaves and putrefying memories. You should not have such a dangerous predator prowling around the house. Can I come inside?" She shouldered past me and immediately went into the kitchen, where she applauded my work on the northern bogflutter and rummaged around for food. "We'll need to bring something to eat."

"Where are we going?"

"Wherever we want. An October day like today is perfect for exploring. I was thinking we should check out the McCallister House, where Gretchen Bottoms used to live."

"Don't know. Doesn't seem like the weather is very nice. It's probably gonna rain more."

She was glowering at the Lady Grimalkin, who was glowering right back. "The McCallister House. That's where we're going. It's empty and haunted and your cat is not invited."

The Lady Grimalkin seemed to sense my mind was made up to go and turned away with a sayonara swishing of her tail.

We headed due east across the island. Temperatures hovered in the low fifties. Clouds dispersed to momentarily allow some peremptory bursts of sunlight—highlighting the reds and oranges of maples, along with the yellows of cottonwoods—but were soon amassing again. River breezes sent more leaves sailing down all around us. She was kicking in the leaves, in a good mood about something. Every now and then she would turn to face me, walking backwards, point her fingers at me and wink. I started kicking in the leaves, too. She was singing some lewd sea shanty about slippery decks and hoisted sails. Every indication pointed to a perfect day.

Unfortunately, the fair weather turned foul. Conditions were rapidly deteriorating and a dramatic scene of churning open water greeted us on East Riverbend. Colder air from the north was colliding with warmer and wetter air from the south and a whirlwind was underway. Felt like the first substantial gale of the season. We started running. The McCallister place—a generously expanded farmhouse which, although now forsaken, retains a dignified air—wasn't that far away. Generations of wildflowers and grasses had made a prairie of the sloping grounds and could be seen swaying and thrashing straight ahead. The two-story house is set farther back from the road and largely concealed by vegetation—groves of ninebark and redbud in particular. She knew where she was going. She was shouting over her shoulder something about deep explorations waiting for us inside as she bounded up on the porch where the front door was wide open, hanging askew and creaking from a broken top hinge.

We entered.

She spoke first. "Let's find someplace private."

The rain outside had been fully unleashed. From upstairs came the echoing sound of interior dripping and splashing. Somewhere a clock was still ticking. We tiptoed down a very dark hallway and passed a framed oil painting of a forest fire on the wall, and a pair of jilted boots on the floor. An umbrella was secured in the corner by the thick web of a wolf spider. Umbrella, boots, human things. In the next room there might be human remains. This was not what she was hoping to find. Instead, she was looking for reading material. Bookcases lining the shadowy interior walls.

The author drifted over and inspected the spines, speculating aloud that these could be the books of Gretchen Bottoms herself. They were definitely older editions. Title by title she became more convinced: *Satanic Lumber Barons: A History,* by Edward Funk; *Hell's Blazes: A Compendium of Personal Accounts of 1870s Conflagrations in the Inland Seas Region,* edited by Rachel Van Horn; *Snowbound Along the Salteaux,* by Celia Vermette; and, of course, *Devil in the Pines,* by the Bottoms family.

She plucked this last title off the shelf.

It was the 1919 edition. "This is her book."

I walked over and peered in the darkness.

"*The Great Horned Owl Murders,* by Olivia Pembroke, sounds exciting. And this one might look familiar." I pulled it gently off the shelf. "*The Supernatural Guide to the Twenty-One Islands of the River of Discards.*"

The sound of a piano being gently played echoed through the house from some deeper den. Just a bar or two, but discernibly a nocturne of some sort. We looked at each other excitedly. Rain lashed the windows.

The piano fell silent.

Simultaneously we detected a resurgent supernatural presence in the rooms around us. There was more than one spirit. The temperature in the house dropped so quickly we heard the audible clicking of water surfaces turning to ice, and saw our breath fog the air.

"Think we better get outta here."

"Good idea."

BOTTLES IN THE CEMETERY

OCTOBER 31

The dying black walnut woke me up this morning. It was more than her usual groaning this time. She was also tapping the window next to the bed with a long branch finger. *Tap-tap-scraaatch*. This was joined by other sounds of movement—mysterious fluctuations and ghostly whispers, the falling of leaves, the exchange of scandalous secrets.

"Halloween," the tree groaned.

My temples throbbed. "I know, I know."

The house was very cold and felt like a damn funeral home. Sitting up in bed felt very much like sitting up in a coffin. It was surprising not to be greeted by funeral wreaths, sympathy bouquets, and shocked mourners. But it was nothing but my same old room, just colder and emptier.

Tap-tap-scraaatch.

I pushed off the sheets and sulked down the hallway. The house had turned desolate, the air thick with the wafting particles of abandonment and decline. Cobwebs dangled like damaged sails. The muted-gray fur of neglect on everything. Candles flickered inexplicably, dancing in the dim air like fool's fire. A skeleton bird chirped in an antique brass birdcage, the hollow bones of which were so tiny and fragile they might have been the inner construction of some type of finch, the beak opening and closing, no song emerging. The only sounds were the distant plucking of a spectral harp and the moaning of an old trombone.

Otherwise, the house was incredibly still.

"Halloween," the black walnut groaned again.

"I heard you."

The Lady Grimalkin, skeptical and hesitant, followed me through the foggy morning, across the fallen leaves. She seemed extremely agitated. Maybe she was remembering some witch in the woods, some witch wherever. Maybe she was growing tired of me all over again. We came across a patch of pumpkins brightening the muck. They had been carved into jack-o'-lanterns on the vine and bore a variety of jagged expressions. Their features were darkened from previous flames, but currently unlit.

My cat paced back and forth, back fur cresting.

"Where the hell did those pumpkins come from?"

She turned and shrugged with a full broomstick arching of her back, but this agitation wasn't intended for me. There were two men walking toward us—two murky silhouettes advancing through the mist in our direction. They both looked vaguely familiar. No one in particular, but rather a slumbrous amalgamation of men I've called friends over the years. Two characters who seemed to have wandered in from a parallel dimension where some other permutation of me resides, warped but recognizable and an acquaintance of theirs. As they drew closer through the shadows, they smiled and hailed me as old companions might, each with a bottle of beer.

The Lady Grimalkin retreated.

"You need to come with us," the stouter and greasier of the two told me.

"You definitely need to come with us," said his skinny and more shifty companion.

"Yeah? Where?"

"The cemetery in the woods."

My unspoken thought was: There sure as hell is no cemetery in these woods.

They looked at each other like conniving brothers and took mirror pulls from their respective bottles. Then the stouter and greasier one spoke again. "There most certainly is."

"We just came from there."

I squinted. "You two look very familiar."

"We should."

"We most certainly should," snickered the greasier one. "Name is Carl."

I nodded. "Sure, Carl."

The skinnier one leaned forward like a tilting, leather-clad mantis, and stuck his hand out. "You can call me Johnny."

Puzzling through the dull haze that permeated everything

resulted in several dragging moments of concentrated silence. "So, you two want me to go to some cemetery?"

"It's not so much the two of us want you, but your lady sure as hell does."

"Drunk in the cemetery." Carl nodded.

"Just like old times." Johnny held up his bottle.

"You comin' or what?"

They drifted back into the trees and I followed. "How far is it?"

"Not very far at all," Johnny sang in hiccups.

"Just another half mile or so."

"Not very far at all," I agreed.

"Told you. Here," said Johnny. "Take this."

He handed me a long-barreled revolver. It was a lot heavier than mine, silver-plated.

"Might want to give that piece a close inspection."

"It's a beauty," said Carl.

"Here." Johnny came up beside me and flipped open his lighter. "Kinda dark with all this fog and shit. This'll help."

The wobbling light of the flame illuminated some of the intricate details. Carvings decorated the barrel all the way down—skulls and flowers and empty liquor bottles—and all were softly moving, swerving around one another, colliding every so often and spinning in opposite directions to collide and spin again. It was mesmerizing.

"What's this for?"

"For you, man."

Johnny nodded and rested a hand on my shoulder. "It's so you can shoot us, if you want us to go."

"What?"

"If you get sick of our bullshit," said Carl.

"Don't worry, it won't hurt us. Just makes us go away."

I accepted this nonsense and looked back down at the gun, but Johnny snapped his lighter closed. "You can stare at it all you want, once we get to the burial grounds. Shouldn't leave your friend waiting. Ain't polite."

They took me into what was no longer familiar woodland, but a haunted forest. In one particularly knotted section of rampant brambles and privet, drooping and dripping leaves turned to face me. Vines coiled. A few looked tropical, similar to the woody climbers that once grew in the great room. My companions did not seem concerned. After a good ten minutes struggling through that mess—Carl and Johnny laughing every so often and pretending to chop at the vegetation with invisible machetes—we arrived at a clearing dominated by a single massive tree, a large oak tree, probably a white swamp oak. There was a dark mound where it sat and strange movement everywhere, including moonglow shapes like reflecting chrome, lifting from the earth as if drawn by an updraft. When I asked my companions what these levitating wisps were, they assured me it was nothing more than swamp gas and laughed again.

"Almost there," said Johnny.

"Just past this old car."

I looked ahead and saw the dark mound, actually an enshrouded mass, in the middle of the clearing, coming into focus. It *was* an old car, looked like a Monte Carlo, and judging by the tree growing directly through the damaged roof, it must have been sitting there for a good forty or fifty years. "This your car?"

Carl coughed. "I had the title, if that's what you mean."

"Parked on the edge of the cemetery forevermore," Johnny crooned.

"Or until the ground turns even more swampy and the whole thing crumbles and gets sucked away. Nothing we ever owned is gonna last forever."

Suppose not, I thought.

"Come on; you thirsty?"

"Sure. Where's the author?"

"Not far."

We skirted a worn footpath on the far side of the rusted hulk and were rewarded with a clear view of the cemetery. The departing mist still smudged the edges. It was small, maybe about twenty or thirty tombstones, all of them at some stage of sinking and collectively resembling rotten teeth, with their mossy surfaces and haphazard tilting.

"Where's Rebecca?"

"Settle down; she'll be back. You still thirsty?"

"I guess so. What is it? No label?"

Carl stooped down by a tombstone where a cooler was placed. "Just beer."

"That works."

He handed me one, then took a bottle of his own. Without labels it seemed suspicious, but didn't taste half bad. It was a very thick and heavy ale with notes of lichen and bark and nicotine. Had the off-kilter intensity of a novice home brew, but it seemed a stretch that either of these characters would attempt such chemistry. Probably something they stole. The more I drank of that heavy ale, the more it shifted taste. Toward the bottom of the bottle there was sediment and a strong flavor of maple syrup.

"That shit went down easy," I told Carl.

"You need another one."

"I think I do."

And for the next two hours we sat there and drank in headlong pursuit of intoxication. We traded stories and talked about music. Johnny had a cassette player with him and tapes stashed in the pockets of his leather jacket, all with cracked cases like junkyard windshields, including some Lady Morticians. We put on the obvious choice for the evening, their first album—*Halloween Greetings from the Lady Morticians*. Must've been an unusually high alcohol content in that brew because standing up to urinate after only three became an issue. I was staggering around and seeing ghosts everywhere, many of them in costume, many of them former sweethearts, enemies, sweethearts with enemies. Of course, I started smoking again.

Johnny had a lot of pockets in his leather jacket and the ones that didn't contain cassettes seemed to conceal packs of cigarettes. By the time the author showed up, my third smoke was halfway to the filter and my condition was completely hammered. She asked if she could borrow my revolver. Forgot I even had the damn thing. "Sure," I said, and handed it over.

"I'm only doing this because you apparently forgot you could," she said, and shot Carl in the head. He vanished.

She turned to look at Johnny, and he knew what was coming. He decided to spend his final moments slicking his hair back. The comb flew out of his greasy hand when the shot went off and he vanished, too.

This kind woman then helped me back through the woods and into the safety of the house.

OBSERVATIONS OF THE RUT TODAY

NOVEMBER 11

There is a scar on Rebecca's shoulder—a glossy white one that wraps all the way across a clavicle, once fractured, which, she initially confided in me, came from a fall near the shores of mighty Lake Manitou. She laughed and said it had been the result of hiking through foul weather with a bottle of cherry wine all by herself. Winds off the big lake knocked her off balance. She fell, over the edge of a steep, wooded moraine—down, down, she chaotically tumbled, eventually thumping into an aspen with a sharp splintering of bone. She was initially stunned. Then came supervening waves of pain, anger, and panic. Rebecca knew better. She broke two of the most basic rules of hiking—first, by heading out alone, and second, by not telling anyone where she was going. Making matters worse was the arrival of a long, slow, forty-degree rain that cleared the trail of hikers. Survival, she realized, was now entirely up to her. Following five uncomfortable minutes of lying on the ground, she decided the weather would only get worse. Finding her vehicle as soon as possible? Clearly the best idea. With this in mind, the careless explorer forced herself up the sturdy base of the unyielding aspen, then stood a moment, summoning the fortitude to deal with the fracture and the bleeding. To deal with it and climb. There were two torturous tumbles along the way, she said, each administering the sharp pain of a fracture being further reconfigured beneath skin that barely contained it. But finally, she reached the top.

Finally, she got to her truck.

That is how I believed the author got her shoulder scar at first. On the fourth night we spent together she told another story, sheepishly informing me it wasn't a moraine tumble at all. She then pointed to the scar and drew my attention to three particular scrapes, asking if they resembled antler swipes. "They should," she said, "because they are." Rebecca then relayed what *really* happened, and it bore little resemblance to the Lake Manitou tale, beyond the presence of wine and the backdrop of the northern woodlands in November. This time, she assured me, it had been some foolhardy taunting of a buck in pursuit of a doe during peak rut. Females in estrus combined with the shifting of the weather had this particular buck in a very agitated and aggressive mood. White-tailed does typically come into estrus for just twenty-four hours, one fleeting day, and a buck in pursuit is a desperate creature. Rebecca's foolish taunting was rewarded with some blows from his ten-point rack.

"Crashed me into the leaves," she went on. "Then stood there, huffing big clouds of exhaust in the frosty air above me for quite some time. After some uncomfortable and tense moments, with mist rising from the heat of my bleeding, this irritable brute regarded me as sufficiently dealt with, cast his nose skyward, scenting his lady, and very simply and very quietly just wandered off."

This encounter is how I believed she got the scar. We even talked about it twice. Each retelling provided new details of the encounter—the dismal trip to the emergency room, her gurney nearly tipped over by an overdosed lunatic yanked free from tubes and creating havoc, the nauseating level of blood loss, the kind nurse in intensive care who smelled of cigarettes and was the sweetest of companions. The long recovery.

Then the story of the scar was modified a third time.

"I did not get this scar because of a deer, either," she confessed just last night. "This scar is the direct result of cavalier fornication. There was once again some cherry wine involved," she said, "but it happened in a family cabin not far from Bogflutter Lake with a man who, over the five years of an unruly and unhealthy relationship, ravished me nearly one hundred times. My greatest lover," she sighed, then went on in pornographic detail about everything that led up to the fracture. It happened with the collapse of a chair and a face-first smacking onto hard cabin floorboards. I listened intently, increasingly dismayed and aroused in equal measure. I knew her old lover wouldn't be in this memory for long. We have reached an unspoken agreement to absorb each other's recollections, to merge them whenever possible and proceed as if we had always been a pair, as if these had always been *our* times. We now smudge away sadly fading faces and replace them with our own.

The author suffers from the same sentimental afflictions as myself. She loves few things more than wallowing around in the past, especially when drinking, but could do without the consequences.

The sighs and the sinking—she knew it was a bad idea, but still had stories to tell. "I want me to be all you have ever known."

"Sounds good to me," was my response, and from that point on we challenged one another, sleeves rolled up, to erect teetering constructions of fabrication—her inventions becoming mine, mine becoming hers, and the one about the shoulder scar and broken bone from so many years ago, as of this morning, now features us holding hands and passing a bottle of whiskey back and forth in some forgotten cemetery where she shot two men.

It had started to rain. The cemetery was a smaller one surrounded by trees, the road leading to it long overgrown, the people buried there long forgotten. Names and epitaphs eroded and anonymous. Caskets compromised by roots, some of them connected by tunneling critters and filled with more scat than bones. There are, of course, campfire stories about the place. Animal sacrifices and crude altars. The feeling of unseen eyes upon you. That cemetery and a frolic with yours truly was where the scar came from now, the result of two tipsy young lovers. A klutzy accident and nothing more.

Earlier today, not long after breakfast, the author abruptly rose and put on her hunting jacket. She told me she was heading down to a little blue house we both knew well, just two miles south on the channel side of the island. She waved me off when I went for my own coat and requested a twenty-minute head start.

"Then what?"

"Then you track me."

I nodded, said, "Well, sure," and watched her go.

Those twenty minutes dragged by.

Most of it was spent anxiously looking out of the window. The sun was still shining, but there were clouds approaching from the northwest and it felt like snow. The twenty-minute mark found me outside and immediately at a light jog, eyes on the sky. Saw a large doe bounding across an overgrown lawn; she paused to consider me for a nervous moment or two, standing in a sea of waving leaves—big, brown oak leaves, combustible red maple leaves—then she sprang away. Moments later, an expected buck emerged from the shadows, ignoring me completely, and trotted the same path as the twitchy doe. He had probably been following her for days, biding his time and fending off other males. He had splashed through puddles and crunched through frost. He had watched her eating berries, and taken berries from the same tree. Her resting periods had become his.

Today, this infatuation draws to a close.

After mating, he will quickly bolt in search of another.

The wind was licking the channel into a rolling procession of whitecaps and gusting straight into my face. A front blowing in straight from the north was carrying the first real snow of the season. Thankfully the little blue house came into view before the storm hit.

The front door had been left wide open.

I stepped up on the creaking porch and turned again to admire the view—windswept waters and lashing white—then went inside, pulling the door shut behind me, locking it.

The sudden quiet of the dark house froze me.

I kept still.

I listened.

Almost complete silence.

The muffled serenity of abandoned places.

The skittering of unseen mice in the walls.

"Rebecca?"

All sounds echoed.

Some dust fell.

Then laughter, *her* laughter.

Moments later I found her in the dank cellar with three candles lit and placed on available high surfaces, shadows dancing all around her. She had a cobwebbed bottle uncorked in her hand. What followed was a conversation that covered lots of ground, including some common ground, like our shared willingness to raise a child in this altered landscape. Our first would be a girl. She would be brave and brilliant. Then there might be a second daughter, or even a fiery-tempered son. Both would prove to bring some trouble to the family—recklessness, hospital stays, criminal records, substance abuse problems, ill-advised relationships—our hair graying prematurely as one day we find ourselves looking into the bathroom mirror, and there, looking back, the haggard reflection of stunned grandparents. It is probably for the best that we only have one, we say. There will be no improving upon her—only insufficient appreciation of her perfection while tending to the troublemakers. An only child, and we will call her something appropriately poetic and, being a worthy heir, allow her to keep the Livingstone name.

Rebecca and I passed that bottle of wine back and forth in the candlelight and she wiped her mouth with the back of her sleeve. She caught the flash in my eye and pressed her lips together in a very feline fashion, and we shared our observations of the rut today. She told me about a buck that emerged suddenly from behind a shagbark hickory and stared her aggressively down, even snorting once.

"I backed away slowly," she said.

WILD-TURKEY DINNER

NOVEMBER 24

The weak light of a cloudy daybreak revealed my bedroom. Familiar for sure, but this morning it felt like a vandalized mausoleum. A new hole appeared in the ceiling overnight, and pouring from this opening were what first appeared to be frayed electrical wires. No plaster debris anywhere. Could've been a cavity formed by a missing light fixture, but no—as my blinking continued and focus improved—the dangling intruders revealed themselves to be roots. Something was growing through the roof. The carrion hawk couldn't quite bring the ceiling down, but this tree or shrub, or whatever it was, would finish the job. The roots, frayed out to a fan of delicate lace at each terminating strand, vacillated slightly in the draft. Cold air poured into the room, crawling over me like spiders. Some scant, clever flurries found their way in. Won't be able to stay in this house very much longer.

The author hadn't been around for quite some time. Three days, three nights. Not egregiously long but long enough to cause some concern she might not return. She left her shotgun leaning by the door. Evidence of a hasty departure. Something must've happened—some injury, some attack. It was probably time to go looking for her, but just as proper attire was being considered, the cat started mewling by the big picture window, and there—emerging from the woods—the author, nose and cheeks red-chafed, eyes glazed from exposure, approaching with lurching steps, leaning forward, shoulders humped. I turned to grab my coat and then saw the birds behind her—three full-grown male turkeys on the far and more congenial side of their mating season, weaving around one another with their fluid, dipping struts and, incredibly, following the author as if she were their mother or prophet. When proceeding at a leisurely gait, the male wild turkey, called a tom, can seem awkward, especially when burdened with the association of its domestic counterparts who have been bred, through hundreds of generations, into cranky but easy prey. Flightless and rotund fools on stunted legs, white feathers drained of camouflage and freedom, gobbling and vocalizing incessantly in suicidal disregard of predators. The wild turkey is an entirely different bird. Instead of being boisterous and foolish, they are clever and evasive. For these three toms to be trailing the author was highly unusual.

She saw me in the window and her acknowledgment was an exhausted but firm nodding. We had to make a meal of at least one of these fat boys. But the uncanniness of the situation, her apparent spell casting, immobilized me. Couldn't tell exactly what she expected, but it didn't seem she wanted me traipsing outside and interfering. Still, the shotgun she'd left behind might come in handy. It was the ideal weapon for felling a turkey, and there was a box of three-inch magnum shells in the laundry room. She didn't have her gun. She might want her gun. Should I get it?

I hesitated, then noticed Rebecca was no longer paying attention to me. She was drawing the birds into the yard with her own plan and it wasn't my place to interfere. The wild turkey has the same naked head as the barnyard variety, but they are much more colorful—dark, woodsy brown and black, with quaking splashes of holiday red wattles. Far from blundering and vulnerable, they are notoriously tricky runners—zigzagging and ducking and shooting off with irritated gobbling in liquid-rapid bolts when necessary. The true wonder of the tom lies not in the iridescence of his impressive fan of tail feathers, but in his breathtaking agility. These birds are also muscular fliers who can flap impressively upon takeoff, ascending with ease on thundering wings, to safer perches in the branches of sturdier trees. In fact, they roost in such trees at night—preferring mature oak, beech, and hickory—especially in the autumn, when these deciduous beauties produce expanding skirts of fallen nuts. The birds behind Rebecca were a solid three feet off the ground and ridiculously plump. As she neared the center of the yard she gently dropped to her knees, slipped a hand inside her jacket, and then—after a slight pause to heave a breath—withdrew her hunting knife just as one of the toms approached curiously from behind, spinning around in one coruscating movement to swipe his head clean off. The other toms flinched and bolted when they witnessed their decapitated companion spurting gouts of blood.

At around lunchtime we stoked a new fire and finished the task of removing the rest of the feathers. Driven by hunger, our preparations were serious, with very little talking for the first hour or so, just methodical movement from station to station inside the house, occasionally noting the thickening flurries outside, but not saying much more. She asked, while pulling the slippery internal organs from the carcass, if we could listen to some music. She straightened up, hands covered in blood, and declared the holiday season officially underway. "It's time for some Christmas music."

We were limited to what we had in my collection and were both disappointed in the titles it lacked. My copy of Johnny Sideburns and the Thigh Ticklers' raunchy classic *Yuletide Ejaculations* was nowhere to be found. Neither was *It's Christmas! Don't Die!* by the Riverbend Stranglers. I did have some jazz and brass bands, but the easy first choice to get us in the holiday spirit was *The Yuletide Demos of Melancholy Adieux*. The opening track is the nearly nine-minute instrumental called "The Melancholy Bells of Christmas." The twangy guitar signatures of Darius Feldspur, the chiming bells played by Karl Lutcher, the twinkling glissandos from the harp of Sara

Bathory Evans, the mournful low-register piano playing of Paderewski, and, in the last two minutes, oscillating bells from who knows where. Few pieces could uncork the yuletide spirit as effectively as that one.

THE SNOWBOUND ISLAND

DECEMBER 18

It's late now, probably close to midnight. Still snowing. The house is very quiet and covered in white. The electricity, after several long, cold months, was restored early this morning and the furnace roared alive with a raucous clang and clamor. This, combined with the irritating brightness of a hallway light left on, is what forced me to open my eyes. The eighteenth of December. One week until Christmas. The Lady Grimalkin stirred from her sleep along with me and was purring loudly at the foot of the bed. She was definitely a yuletide cat, expecting the month to provide ribbons and wrappings and empty boxes to investigate. Warm fires and fireside blankets. Music and lights.

Getting out of bed wasn't easy, but it happened. The cat softly thudded to the floor. She meowed. The unexpected heat pouring from the vents turned the air in the house foggy and some of the draftier windowpanes could be heard crackling. There was also the accompanying harsh, burnt smell of a furnace lurching into begrudging action after a long dormancy. It smelled acrid and infernal. Soot seemed to spread like moss up those lower vents during the warmer months and they were long overdue for a proper cleaning. This was how the smell of the bellsnickle was described to me—like old furnaces just come to life, and soot.

The Lady Grimalkin seemed upset, but the return of heat was good news to me. It also meant the return of incandescent light. I tried every switch in the house. Everything, as of today, seemed to be working. Then more holiday music, louder than before—the Melancholy Adieux one more time, followed by Big John Stillwater's *Rockabilly Christmas*. Remembered boxes of old holiday lights were brought in from the garage, trailing long cobwebs. Nearly all of them still worked, too. Also in the garage was the old fake tree. The iron wires of its branches needed some reshaping, but were pretty easy to bend once they thawed out a bit. I gave the tree a hearty throttle and a dazed mouse dropped to the concrete floor. The tiny rodent limped off behind the lawnmower. Outside it was still snowing.

Once the tree was in the house and respectably configured, I hung ornaments with their scraggly hooks, spun lights from their tightly wrapped wheels, festooned old Tannenbaum from top to bottom, then plugged it in. My decorating lasted until nightfall because there was plenty more stowed away in the garage that was salvageable—like shimmering blue icicle lights that needed to be secured along the gutters, and even some glowing presents that could be placed in their customary arrangement in front of the blue spruce, and that funny little dented snowman which always looked tipsy and ready to fall. During all of this, it kept right on snowing—lumping on my shoulders and winter cap—and every so often there came a howling in the distance that reminded me of wolves. Then the wintry breeze would wipe the air clear with a vanishing hiss and all would be peaceful again.

My manic assembly of lights continued in the elements until night fell and the snow turned into a blizzard, transforming the island into the glistening wonderland of a shaken snow globe. The solstice is best when it buries us deep. It will take more subzero weeks for the straits to freeze, but the canals and coves and shallows are coated in ice and covered in several inches of fresh white. Marshes and their tall reeds have been drained to the color of tinder, locked in rigid place with their feathertops shuddering. Conditions are harsh.

Most animals have taken shelter, but not the tundra swan. In flocks of several dozen, they float in the open waters south of the main island, largely unfazed, even taking flight in smaller formations through the swirling flakes, their shivering high-register calls coming through in waves. Tundra swans are very close in appearance to our native trumpeter swan, but lack the yellow teardrop smear on the black bill. In a handful of months they will be flying north again to breed on the landscape they're named after—a sparse termination of the boreal forest where the subsoil is permanently frozen. In the open stretches and along the remote shorelines beneath curtains of northern lights and curving skies, they will build their nests while the wind whistles and blows. There they will lay eggs and rear their young. Tundra summer is their reward—the still cold but endless days when the blowing subsides a bit and the wildflowers explode.

Northern cardinals arrived at the feeder just before dusk. Cardinals are frequent backyard visitors all year long, but the white simplicity of winter suits them best because, when all the bright-colored migrants of summer have departed and those which stayed behind have adopted more solemn coloration for the dreary months, the male northern cardinal remains enthusiastically red. The birds who visited the feeder today were a breeding pair, attracted not only by the food but by the lights all plugged in and bright—our house a solitary beacon of glad tidings in an otherwise desolate township. The northern cardinal sets a fine example for couples to emulate. No matter the season, they visit the feeders and, once they have formed a bond, are almost always seen together. They converse back and forth. They sing to one another. The two at the feeder today were singing quietly until the male dropped and opened his wings as if preparing to conduct some courtship dance. Instead, he used those wings to smear the bloody color from his feathers onto the snow in the shape of a heart. The heat of the applied color caused the painted shape to sink. The female hopped down to look, and, when the hole was deep enough, she leapt into the heart and vanished. The male, pausing only for a quick territorial glance around, lifted in flight and wheeled quickly downward in pursuit of his partner. A light rumbling shook the snowy landscape and moments later a fountain of northern cardinals erupted from the hole and poured upwards through the trees and blowing snow, males and females both, forming ribbons skyward. After dozens flapped up from the heart-shaped hole, it quickly filled with snow until the white was once again seamless. No way of telling anything had ever been there at all.

It might keep snowing all month. Snowing even when breaks in the clouds reveal the blue radiance of a moon. Snowing even when we sleep, softly piling on the rooftop above and forming tufted heaps along the gutters. It is suddenly winter, suddenly beautiful. How sad are the islands never skirted in ice and lavished with snowfalls. How sad are the islands on the consistently balmy side of things that never hush themselves as comprehensively as this. The serenity of lapping waves all frozen in place. The creaking silence of everything when the wind dies down.

"What are you thinking?"

"Nothing, really."

"What were you thinking?"

My response sounded embarrassing out loud. "I like the creaking silence of everything when the wind dies down."

She nodded. "I agree."

"Did we have children?"

"I believe we did; a little girl."

"Just the one?"

"Just the one."

"She seems to have stayed little."

"That's right. She is never more than eight years old at Christmas. She's here somewhere."

My eyes closed. "Glad we got those lights up."

"It was mostly you, mister." Her voice trailed off into unreachable fathoms and my eyes reopened to a festive place. The tree garishly decorated. Most of the ornaments were familiar—the red-nosed reindeer from a long-ago holiday season spent all snowed in at Welldigger Bay College, the snowman with the carrot nose picked out in that little shop in a long forgotten small town nestled against an interior lake. The man behind the counter there had a name tag that said Brian, and there was a fresh bruise on his forehead and a cheap wedding band pinching the flesh of a sausage-red finger. Funny the things you remember.

Some of the tree ornaments were even animated with a kind of squirming half-life—tiny elves and caribou and such. One of the elves navigated in an ungainly way on spindly insect legs down the tree, sending delicate glass ornaments swaying, until finally landing on a present with those spindly legs bent backward like a grasshopper. Shortly after landing, he unzipped his hunter-green felt pants with the white fur trim and pissed.

"I see you decorated the tree."

She nodded and laughed at the elf. "Mischievous little fuckers."

"You wrapped presents?"

"Well, you certainly didn't help. You've been passed out there for hours."

She was older now, with childbirth hips and strands of gray. "Seems like I've been here longer than that."

She shook her head. "It's only been a couple hours. I was just going to wake you, though."

The elf had finished his long release and the musky urine smell wafted off the desecrated gift in a visible jaundiced cloud. He seemed satisfied and smiled broadly before crawling away to hide among the brightly wrapped boxes and bows. Everything about his movements suggested a pest.

"Where's the cat?"

"Locked in the guest room until our little helpers leave."

I listened and could faintly hear scratching, followed by a mewling growl. The Lady Grimalkin heard my voice. She wanted out.

"I hope you don't mind, but we're having visitors."

I looked down at what I was wearing. "Not sure I'm ready for guests. What guests?"

“’Tis the season to make amends.”

“With who? Elves?”

“Of course, with the elves, but not just them. Other old familiar faces. Even the bellsnickle will be around later, when it’s time for the elves to go. Sometimes they don’t leave quietly and things get messy, but no worries, the cardinals you saw earlier will return in the moonlight to clean the blood from the snow. To pull its redness back into their wings.”

“The bellsnickle?”

The bellsnickle had darkened the three most magical Christmas seasons of my youth—when I was five and six and seven. Stories told to me by elders in the reliably appropriate ambience of candles and strings of multicolored lights. My grandparents always had a real tree, which meant there were always needles on the floor. The sun always fell before five. The snow piled up outside and Grandma spun yarns about the plague of bellsnickles she encountered during her youth overseas. Sinister creatures all covered in snow-encrusted fur, wearing necklaces of sleigh bells, toting a switch and a flash of teeth that were too lengthy and tapered and white. The helpers of Saint Nicholas. The necessary punishers of bad children. Grandma told me in great detail how this creature announced his presence to her with the eerie tapping of a slender, dead branch against her bedroom window. Huddled beneath the covers with her sisters, she saw that face leering in the frosted pane amid snowy darkness and the constant smell of something burning.

The bellsnickle only lost his ability to trouble my holiday dreaming when my belief in Santa Claus was cruelly extinguished at the age of nine. Holidays following those devout years became characterized by an immediate emptiness, signaling the cold, drafty realities of adulthood not far away. Things would never be the same. Grandma's stories had been so vivid and were told with such old-country conviction, but really were all just made up. Christmas became a hollow and sad thing, but not forever. Nothing is forever.

"You used to have nightmares about him dragging his dirty sack through the snow just outside your window—humming familiar carols, his necklace of bells resembling a harness of skulls in the moonlight. The bellsnickle will pay us a visit tonight, but not to punish us, I promise. It's just to get rid of the elves."

It became clear these creatures were brethren to the lone imp of the black walnut. Each with the same dreadful green eyes, the same rasping laughter. Moments later an arachnid waterfall of them poured from the decorated tree where they had been hidden the whole time. They were all laughing, a mocking and savage chorus—easily over twenty of them. Once on the hardwood they scampered to form an uneasy circle around me. Rebecca, features now fogged and ashen, stood just beyond and reared her arms halfway, like an exhausted oracle.

"They will not hurt you."

Looking around me at those spasmodic bodies and all those tiny heads filled with sharp teeth reminded me of just how perilous my situation was. "Are they the ones who wrapped all these presents?"

She nodded.

"Maybe even helped with the cookies…"

"And tended the fire. But it appears our little party is drawing to a close because, well, you're waking up."

THE UNFAMILIAR DOOR

DECEMBER 21

This morning there were strange reverberations bubbling out into the open air and bringing something aromatic along with them. A drifting scent, some kind of heavily applied essence of mulled wine. This was definitely not the damn bell-snickle. This was some solstice visitation where the purpose could very well be carrying my ass off for good. A rush of fragrances, and some odors, filled the room as bright as a sunrise and a warm figure delicately settled next to me, bedsprings reacting with a muted whine. Then the tapered fingers of a frail hand. Then white-out conditions. Then scenes from long ago. My wife was there. My daughter was there. Family milling about. Strings of lights twinkling on spruce boughs. They were in the kitchen, and their voices could be heard as soon as the door was opened. I stomped the snow off my boots in the entranceway. Those shitty boots. It was a ten-inch snowfall, and a long time ago.

The memory left me standing in the kitchen with no damn idea how I got there. The furnace was laboring. The house felt cold. Silky webs decorated the blender and the great room was still in disarray from our party, from the elves or imps or whatever they were. Most of the decorations had been knocked off the tree and some of the lower branches were blackened above a scorched spot on the floor where combustible presents had been set ablaze. The fireplace was dark, inactive, and something was wedged inside. A quick investigation revealed the cooked carcass of what appeared to be a pheasant and some random silverware—the whole mess blackened with soot. Evidence of some feasting, some ruckus.

Now all was still.

The snowy landscape outside the picture window.

The house not even whispering.

Every so often a disappointed bird flapped in to investigate the empty feeders, hanging crooked on rusty chains like busted remnants from a torture chamber, all creaked with corrosion and blood.

None of those birds stuck around. Neither did I.

Following an afternoon of sleep, I woke up trembling. The sun was gone and the house was frigid, darkness settling in for the next fifteen hours.

Not entirely dark, of course.

The sky outside was clear—the moon swollen, nearly full, and casting an old-television luster. Stars everywhere. From the great room the sound of a hearty masculine laugh rang out and a new fire burst from the hearth—a vivacious blaze that scorched the remnants of the pheasant. The house instantly felt like a hunter's den smelling of cooked meats and spices. From some unseen distance came the upbeat chatter of drunken voices. The wavering ceiling shadows suggested antlers. Soon the voices faded, along with the laughter. At least the fire was still burning, but it needed tending and the dining room window had been left open. Snow tracks were left on the carpet. Most were from birds, but others belonged to what could only have been some kind of weasel, maybe the ermine. Windows were open in the kitchen, too. Snow all over the floor. That's where the weasel tracks took me—scanning for something snarling and slippery, but instead finding an unceremonious end to those tracks, where the snowy imprint of great horned owl wings and tail feathers marked a deadly strike. The ragged talon hole in the middle was decorated with a necklace of blood and there was an additional bright speckling, as if someone fanned a dripping red paintbrush across the floor. The unfortunate critter, whatever it was, had suffered arterial damage and the successful predator could be satiated, but nearby. A few feathers were left behind, animated restlessly by the cold air. There were no hoots.

My search for the bird took me into the office. The office used to have two windows, but today there was only an unfamiliar door—formed on the south wall where a framed map of Lake Manitou used to hang. A clammy wetness glistened on the surface, and it was bulging. The wood heavy and old. The knob sooty black and infernal. The powerful iron hinges holding it in place seemed to have retained the warmth of their final forging and radiated faintly. This ancient door had just happened. I reached out to turn the knob, then paused to marvel at my frigid hand with the blue bones visible—blue bones pressing up against papery cadaver skin—then considered the knob, which still appeared to be alive with a gentle throbbing heat, but darkening, hardening. I hesitated.

Best to get some gloves. Thankfully there were some in the corner on top of the filing cabinet. There were also some old photos up there. Most were in pretty bad shape after a year spent in hastily packed boxes under dripping eaves. There were a few of my father. A few of my father and me. I quickly grabbed the gloves, went back to that doorknob, and twisted it with purpose. It made a dull double thunk, coughed out a sulfurous chimney puff, then opened. Without hesitation I stepped through. Heard the crunch of snow beneath my feet. The hurried rush of midwinter air.

I was outside. Some nocturnal outside. Some enchanted yuletide outside. The trees were mostly towering conifers backlit by the green cascading swirls of northern lights. There was a silent caravan of moose in the moonlight across the snow, the steam of exertion sainting their racks with wispy halos. There were youngsters in the ranks. A moose calf weighs around thirty pounds when born and can eventually top a thousand as an adult. This group was surviving winter on a diet of twigs and buds, cutting a browse line through the woods. They didn't seem to notice me. The breeze, light but blowing into my face, probably helped. Not moving a muscle also probably helped. They couldn't smell me and sure as hell couldn't see me, so my challenge was to stay quiet until they passed. Moose survive the winter, but don't like it. They would rather be in the cool waters of summer lakes and ponds, munching on long, dripping strands of green. They are accomplished swimmers and can gallantly take on the challenges of a deeper river. They moved into the trees—the festive white spruce, towering white pine, ancient white cedar—and went elsewhere.

My eyes caught spooky, flickering red lights coming from some deeper habitation. A rustic lodging with a chimney sending up smoke. And fuck, was it cold. All was still, not even the slightest disturbance of wind. But, turning to look north across the massive lake, I saw a line of mounting darkness, a blizzard on the way.

Might be the type to last for three days straight.

Not the time to be caught way out here.

The column of chimney smoke became my new destination. Snowshoes and a much weaker force of gravity allowed me to bound along on great soaring leaps, each ending with a muffled thump of impact, a skier's bended crouch, then a thrust back up and out into the air again. Each powdery stride was longer and more productive than the last. This mode of travel got me to that little cabin with the smoking chimney in no time. In fact, crossing that distance resulted in momentum that made it difficult to stop. My snowshoes skidded across the porch and slammed concussively into the front door. The hat on my head flipped off. Everything turned to ink.

Consciousness found me back in the office, returned right into my chair. No unfamiliar door, just two old drafty windows. The house restored. The furnace running again.

And something else.

Maybe nothing more than the crinkly and niveous hisses of ice forming, but it really sounded like something else.

Seemed a deliberate tapping, very faint at first.

Windowpane tapping.

The clicking of pointed nails or claws on glass coming from the living room. And another sound in the distance—wind chimes or other bells, reverberating through the snowy breezes, muffled by all the falling white but unmistakably reverberating through. The gloomy cloaked figure of the bell-snickle, his sack of sorrows dragging across the snow. He had peered in as if checking up on me, and, disappointed to find me still alive, just carried on. Felt sorry for the creature to be out on a night like this, but no way in hell was he coming into the house. My concern was that when he dumped the heartrending contents of his bag out and the moonlight animated them, it would be impossible to look away.

THE FROZEN RIVER OF DISCARDS

DECEMBER 31

The River of Discards is locked in ice from shore to shore, snow heaped everywhere and molded by the wind into drifts. Everything incredibly still.

Every now and then a deep seismic crunch from ice far below reconfiguring, lengthening—but little else. Coursing aimlessly along just three feet above the ice was a particularly large bank of white, and we crashed into it with a thundering puff, holding hands.

Hers so small and sweaty.

Nails digging in.

The sound of breaking glass in the darkness. The wet coppery smell of mortal injuries. The delicate float of flurries in the stunned silence. The distant approach of sirens. Eventually. But these were sounds only faintly heard through the humming darkness. Also present were pangs of unimaginable shame.

Then a burning retch of blood followed by floating oblivion. When my eyes reopened, there was a spot for me on an early afternoon barstool, motes in the air and Big Tom Wellwater on the jukebox. The bartender—damn if I can remember his name—was watching me with concern, a lighter in his hand. "You gonna be all right?"

"Probably not," I remember telling him.

"You need a light?"

At that moment, two things occurred to me. The first was the presence of an unlit cigarette in my mouth. The second was that my cheeks were wet with tears. I had been making a damn fool of myself again. My old fishing rod was leaned on the bar, and a bucket, also clearly mine, sat on the floor. The bucket had a single black bullhead moping in the bottom, making me feel even worse.

I was walking along the shore at the very tip of the island where the long expanse of the big lake begins, and there on the shoals was the shipwreck of a many-masted schooner all locked in ice and stranded. The moonlight and the whistling of its tattered masts formed into a fibrous, misty cloud. This cloud in turn became a cold fog, with trees emerging from it in full autumnal color. Sunlight above, and the cold fog was breaking. The trail was a familiar one, winding around hardwood-forested moraines and ending on the sandy beaches of a bay on Lake Laurentide. Leaves crunching as we walked along, our daughter taking the lead, swinging an empty bag that would soon be filled with beach stones.

The air felt warm and steamy from storms just rolled through, thunder still rumbling in the distance, and we were on the hunt for caterpillars when we saw the amazing hummingbird moth instead. My daughter either fed off my excitement or generated her own, but I remember how she held an arm up to keep me at bay so she could make her approach. The hummingbird moth was searching around like its rapid wing-beating namesake near open blooms of wild bergamot. We watched as it unfurled its long, coiled proboscis, hovering and stationary. It had a tongue twice as long as its body. She looked up at me and the heat of the day increased. The sunlight turned blinding. Through the squinting brightness came the outline of trees, along with the island they were attached to. It was autumn and they were dropping their brilliant orange leaves across the damaged pavilion. The maple trees were now black walnuts, leafless and spilling their branches upward, lifting to disappear in clouds getting darker by the moment.

No boat was in the slip, just a single sad suitcase left behind filled with children's clothes. We pitched the whole thing into the waves to rid ourselves of its oily sadness, then kissed and stripped away layers. Something was moving out on the blustery river. The figure initially impressed me as something human, gently paddling a canoe through the rainy waters. Emerging details suggested otherwise. This beastie had sinewy arms that seemed a trifle too long. It was definitely a *him*. The arched fluidity of his rowing suggested some unnatural feline lineage, and the lowered head conducted a predatory scan of the water and shoreline until, for a moment, his yellow eyes locked with mine. He smiled like a salamander, then vanished into the mist.

Outside it was snowing again, and from the murky darkness of the woods, there was movement—a procession of some sort, all solemn and bowed. In the lead was a more famished and decrepit bellsnickle, openly weeping, followed by shrouded figures with faces decomposed nearly down to the bone, jaws clacking dry. They were flanked by canines which restlessly roved the perimeter—*Canis lupus*, the gray wolf. Long, bushy tails dipped in black ink. The otherwise white snout dipped in black ink, sometimes dripping red. There were five in this guardian pack, and when the bellsnickle dropped into the snow from depletion they all raised their faces and howled. Then, faces in the window—two faces. Five stories up. Two faces in the wintry darkness, and they seemed to be in hushed and excited conversation. Then I recognized her.

Bob Stevens is a librarian at Eastern Michigan University.

www.ingramcontent.com/pod-product-compliance
Lightning Source LLC
Chambersburg PA
CBHW030533310726
48979CB00010B/1897/J
* 9 7 8 1 9 6 5 2 7 8 2 9 1 *